D1415359

BEDTIME TALES

Linda Jennings
Illustrated by Hilda Offen

Cathay Books

For Shirin and Karen
and
Emily Katherine Vickers

This edition first published in 1989 by
Octopus Books,
Michelin House,
81 Fulham Road,
London SW3 6RB.
Reprinted 1990
© Copyright Octopus Books Limited 1989
ISBN 0 7064 3703 9
Printed and bound in Hong Kong

Contents

Bulb Time

'It's snowing,' said Matthew. 'How awful.'

'I thought you liked snow,' said Dad.

'Not in March,' said Matthew. 'Not when all the bulbs I planted last fall are just about to come up.'

'Snow won't hurt them,' said Dad. 'It acts as a blanket. They'll be all right, you'll see.'

But the next day the snow lay thick over the ground.

'I can't see *any* of my bulbs,' said Matthew. 'All the green shoots have disappeared!'

At lunchtime the sun came out and some of the snow melted away. The next day it was still sunny. Matthew went to see his garden. 'Dad!' he cried.

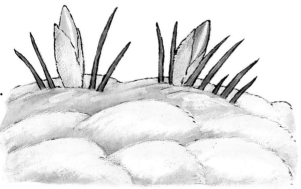

Through the snow poked two crocuses, one yellow and one purple.

'Told you so!' said Dad.

5

Fairground Fun

When Penny went to the fair she didn't look at the giant slide or the bumper cars. She turned away from the ghost train and the tilt-a-whirl. She always liked to go home with something she'd won. Last time it had been a goldfish. This time she'd set her heart on a green china vase from the ring toss booth. She wanted to give it to Mom for her birthday, but she only had 50 cents left. What would happen if she didn't win it after all? And Mom was standing right beside her!

'What a horrible-looking vase,' said Mom. 'Whoever would want to win *that*!'

'Oh,' said Penny sadly.

'Do you know,' said Mom dreamily, 'there's something I've always wanted to do for years.'

'What's that?' asked Penny.

'Go on a really old-fashioned merry-go-round,' said Mom. 'On one of those ostriches.'

Penny smiled. 'I'll treat you,' she said.

'Great!' said Mom.

So Mom climbed onto an ostrich and Penny sat astride a splendid horse with flaring nostrils, and round and round and up and down they went waving to all their friends.

'Much more fun than winning things,' said Penny, as the ride finally came to an end.

'Mmm,' agreed Mom. 'Thank you for a lovely birthday treat.'

A Spaceman in the Yard

'**D**addy, there's a spaceman in the yard,' cried Lisa.

Daddy was vacuuming the living room. 'Oh yes?' he said. 'Watch your feet, Lisa.'

'Mommy, there's a spaceman on the grass,' repeated Lisa.

But Mommy was washing dishes in the kitchen and didn't have her glasses on. 'Don't be silly, darling. It's the birdbath.'

Lisa went out onto the grass. The spaceman was only very little, so she wasn't afraid. The spaceship seemed to have hit the birdbath and nose-dived into a flower bed.

'Hello, I'm Lisa,' she said politely. 'Can I help you?'

The spaceman pointed to the little spaceship and chattered excitedly.

'Oh, I see. You want me to get it out of the flower bed for you.'

Lisa lifted the spaceship as easily as a toy airplane. 'There you are,' she said. The little spaceman walked to the door of his craft and waved goodbye.

'Don't track dirt on the carpet,' said Daddy as Lisa came in. 'Oh, look, Lisa, there's some kind of bird flying over the fence – or perhaps it's a flying saucer,' he joked.

'Perhaps it is,' said Lisa.

Halloween Pumpkin

Frank's dad was growing a pumpkin. It was simply enormous, but no one knew what to do with it. 'We could have pumpkin pie,' said Frank's dad, 'but Mom's lost the recipe, and anyway, I hate it.'

'We could put the pumpkin in a show,' suggested Frank. But there was only a flower show in town, and they didn't want prize pumpkins.

'It's a white elephant,' sighed Dad, 'it's completely useless.' Suddenly, Mom had an idea.

The next night was Halloween, and the family had a party in the yard. Frank dressed up as a ghost, Mom put on a witch's hat and Dad made everyone dunk for apples. And, lighting up the whole scene, was a simply enormous jack-o'-lantern!

Little Spider

Little Spider felt very upset. 'Nobody loves me,' he said. 'People love baby kittens and puppies and ducklings, but nobody loves baby spiders!' He knew he was right. Bobby Briggs had just put Little Spider down Emma's neck. 'Take that horrible thing away,' she had screamed. 'I *hate* spiders.'

Now Little Spider could see Emma coming along the road to school.

'Ooh,' she cried spotting his web. 'How pretty! Just like a little lace hat.'

Little Spider felt very proud. It was his own, special, dew-spangled design that he had spun that very morning.

'Clever Little Spider!' said Emma. 'I'll never be afraid of you again!'

The Lion's Escape

The lion wanted to escape from the zoo. He was tired of all those faces peering through the bars at him and although he had a nice enclosure with trees to scratch on there was not much space to roam around.

One day a cat came to visit him at the zoo.

'I wish I had an enclosure like yours with trees to sharpen my claws on,' said the cat. 'I'm not allowed to scratch anything at home.'

The lion thought the cat's home sounded rather cosy. According to the cat, he had a big furry rug, a fireplace and a squashy armchair.

'Let's change places,' said the lion.

So the lion made his way to the apartment building where the cat lived, and climbed up the fire escape to the back door.

'I can't take *you*,' said the cat's owner. 'You're much too big. You'd eat a hundred cans of cat food a week. And if you lay on the hearth I wouldn't see the fire at all.'

In the zoo's enclosure, the cat was trying to find a private spot. Cats like to be private. But everywhere he looked he could see faces, and he missed his squashy armchair. 'I'm going home,' he said.

The lion padded back to the zoo, where he met the zookeeper.

'Guess what?' said the zookeeper. 'Tomorrow you go to live in a safari park. There'll be plenty of space for you there!'

Dog in the Manger

Aesop

There was once a dog who decided to live in a manger. This annoyed the horses very much. For dogs eat bones and meat, and are not the slightest bit interested in eating grain and oats and all the things that horses enjoy. But this miserable dog growled at the poor horses who tried to get to their food.

'Why can't the wretched dog let us be?' asked the horses. '*He* doesn't want our food, and shouldn't be living here anyway. Yet he keeps us away from what is rightfully ours.'

The Wolf and the Crane

Aesop

A wolf once swallowed a bone, which got stuck in his throat. He was in agony, and promised to give a big reward to anyone who would take it out for him.

Because the wolf was an untrustworthy creature, many animals refused to help. But at last the wolf persuaded a crane to help him. She put her long neck down the wolf's throat and pulled out the bone.

'And what will be my reward?' asked the crane.

The wolf laughed heartily. 'Why, the fact that I haven't eaten you up, you stupid creature,' he said, as he walked away.

You should never expect anything from rascals, for you are sure to be disappointed.

The Hare and the Tortoise

Aesop

The hare was always boasting that he could run faster than any other animal. So when the tortoise challenged him to a race, the hare laughed his head off. 'Of course,' he said graciously, but to himself he said: 'This will be so easy for me that I can safely take a nap on the way.'

The day of the race arrived, and the two animals set off. Soon the hare decided to stop for a snooze. Why, the tortoise had only just passed the starting line!

The sun rose higher. The hare slept on, but the tortoise plodded ahead, his thick shell protecting him from the sun. By late afternoon the tortoise only had six feet to go to the finishing post!

Suddenly, the hare woke up and realized it was nearly dark! He jumped up and ran and ran – but too late! The tortoise had beaten him!

So it is that the slow, steady ones are often the ones that achieve their goal.

Percy's Journey

It was spring-cleaning day and Percy the Cat knew that meant trouble: his favorite sunning spot disturbed, that horrible vacuum cleaner roaring round his feet, and wet soap-suds flecking his orange fur.

Percy decided to find somewhere quiet where he could curl up into a tight ball until it was all over. He walked outside the gate and saw the ideal place: a large armchair in the back of a truck. Percy trotted up the ramp, curled up on the cushion and was soon fast asleep.

When he awoke it was dark, and the chair was shaking. The truck was moving very fast. Percy crouched down on the cushion, hoping it would stop. It did – and Percy suddenly saw daylight again. He dashed down the ramp and onto a completely strange sidewalk. Where was his green gate, and the oak tree outside? 'I'm lost,' thought Percy. Then he thought, 'A cat is never lost. A cat can *always* find his way home.'

So Percy twitched his tail, turned his nose northward and started walking home. Two weeks later, when his little pads were worn sore and his stomach was empty, Percy suddenly saw his own green gate and his oak tree with a notice on it. It said:

'Lost – orange cat.'

'I'll never mind spring-cleaning day again!' said Percy, curling up on his favorite sunning spot.

Top Floor Tommy

Tommy lived near the top of a big apartment building. From his window he could see right down to the playground at the bottom. There he could see some children, no bigger than toy soldiers, playing on the swings and the merry-go-rounds. There was one girl who looked really fun. She slid down the slide backward, she stood on her head and she threw a ball so high that it almost reached Tommy's window. Tommy wanted more than anything in the world to be that girl's friend but his mom said he was too young to go out on his own.

'But I don't have any friends,' said Tommy.

'It takes time,' said Mom. Mom, Dad and Tommy had only lived in the building for a month. They didn't know anybody.

Tommy tried to make the children notice him. He banged on the window, he threw a plastic duck down into the playground. But the children didn't even look up.

One Saturday afternoon, Tommy and Dad were watching football on television while Mom was out. When she came back she had two visitors with her.

'We met on the bus,' explained Mom. 'This is Mrs Paterson, and this is Jeanie.'

Tommy grinned. Jeanie was the girl from the playground, and she was coming to play! Jeanie smiled at Tommy, and Tommy knew they were going to be the best of friends.

Jack and the Beanstalk

There was once a boy called Jack who was sent to market to sell his mother's cow. When he returned he gave his mother five beans instead of any money. 'I've been told that these will make our fortune,' said Jack, but his mother was furious. She threw the beans out of the window and sent Jack to bed without his supper. When Jack woke up the next morning he saw an enormous beanstalk towering high into the sky, through the clouds. Jack sprang out of bed, opened the window and climbed up that beanstalk in a trice. When he poked his head through the clouds, he was amazed to discover a huge castle. 'This must be where my fortune lies,' cried Jack, and he ran toward it.

A frightened old lady opened the door. 'Go away,' she cried. 'A giant lives here and he eats boys for breakfast!' But Jack slipped into the room and hid himself carefully. Presently the giant appeared with a huge sack of gold coins. He started to count them, but soon dropped asleep. Jack sneaked out of his hiding place, swept the coins into the sack, and set off down the beanstalk again. When the giant awoke he ran after Jack, and started to climb down the beanstalk. As soon as Jack reached the bottom he cut down the beanstalk, giant and all. The giant died, and Jack and his mother lived off the gold coins to the end of their days.

Aunt Mabel's Hat

Aunt Mabel had a splendid hat. It was made from red and black velvet with a bunch of cherries on it. She was very proud of it.

One day Aunt Mabel took her nephew and niece to the zoo.

'Please wear your hat,' said Timothy.

'And your coat to match,' said Anne.

They visited the lions and the monkeys, the bears and the parrots. They were just walking down the path towards the panda's cage when Aunt Mabel's hat suddenly lifted off her head. She looked up and saw it high in the air, quite beyond her reach, in a giraffe's mouth!

Aunt Mabel waved her umbrella. 'You naughty giraffe,' she cried. 'Give me back my hat at once.'

And because the giraffe couldn't eat the cherries, he did!

Fairground Fish

David won a fish at the fairground. He took it home in a plastic bag. It looked very unhappy. It had nowhere to swim. Mom put it in the sink, but David knew it couldn't stay there. Then Uncle Len came over to ask if David would help him clear out his shed. There was lots of junk in it – old bicycle tires, flower-pots, a broken radio – and an aquarium! It needed a bit of paint on the rusty parts, but otherwise it was fine.

'Just right for my fairground fish,' said David.

The Face in the Water

Once, long ago in Greece, there was a very beautiful and vain young man. One hot day he sat down by a pool and gazed into its depths. He saw a handsome face looking up at him.

'Oh how beautiful you are!' he said to the face, and he could not drag himself away. He sat there all day and all night and then the next day and night. He grew thin and pale, but still he sat there, gazing. At last the man grew so weak that he faded away altogether, and where he had sat, there grew a narcissus – a snow-white flower with a little golden face – which nodded and bobbed in the breeze to its reflection in the water.

Hedgehog Brush

When Thomas let the cat out one dark and windy night, he noticed an old brush lying in the porch.

'Dad must have left it there after cleaning the car,' he thought. He was just closing the door when Susan said: 'There's a funny noise out there, a sort of snuffly noise.'

Both children opened the door wide and peered out.
'Look at that old brush!' cried Thomas. 'It moved!'
'It's not a brush, silly,' said Susan. 'It's a hedgehog!'
'I bet it's hungry,' said Thomas. 'Let's get it some bread and milk.'
And so they did.

The French Bread

Jean-Paul lived in a small village in France. Every morning his mother would send him to the bakery to buy some crusty bread. French bread is very long and thin, like a stick, so Jean-Paul would tuck the bread under his arm and walk home with it, reading a comic book at the same time.

Bon-bon also lived in the village. Bon-bon was a large and very greedy dog. One morning he saw Jean-Paul coming home with his French bread, and Bon-bon's mouth drooled. He padded slowly along behind the boy, and 'snap!' he had bitten off the end of the bread. Yummy! It was delicious! Another 'snap!' and half the bread was gone. But Jean-Paul didn't notice. He had just reached the most exciting bit of the comic book where the aliens had landed. 'Crunch-crunch, that was very good,' thought Bon-bon. 'Just one more bit, and that still leaves a tiny piece for Jean-Paul to take home for breakfast!'

When Jean-Paul reached home, his mother was looking as fierce as the alien. 'Next time you go to the bakery, leave your comic book at home,' she said. 'And Bon-bon may as well have the last piece, too.'

'It pays for a dog to be naughty,' thought Jean-Paul. 'But not a small boy!'

A Visit to the Dentist

Rasheed had a broken tooth. It didn't hurt him too much at first, so he pretended nothing was wrong. He was frightened of going to the dentist.

That night, he woke up crying with pain.

Mom took him along to the dentist the very next day.

'Open up!' said the dentist. Rasheed felt a tiny pin-prick, and then, wonderful! No more pain.

'O.K?' smiled the dentist. 'We've fixed your tooth.' She gave Rasheed a tube of pink-striped toothpaste and a button with a happy smiling face on it, just like Rasheed's!

The Balloon Race

Griselda Goblin was taking little Gerry to a fair in Goblin Village. They each had six groobles to spend. (Groobles is goblin money.) First Griselda took Gerry on the roller coaster, then they had a try at the pitching booth. 'We've got two groobles left,' said Griselda. 'What would you like to do?'

'I'd like a balloon,' said Gerry.

'Why, it's a balloon race,' said Griselda. 'And the prize is ten groobles.'

Griselda bought a blue balloon and Gerry a yellow. They wrote their names on the balloons. Then they let go of them. The balloons went sailing up in the sky.

Later that week Gerry received a card. 'My balloon went the furthest,' he said excitedly.

'Ten groobles would buy us each a ticket to Cockleshell Bay,' said Griselda. 'We could have a day by the sea!'

And so they did.

Hidden Hamster

Someone had let Dipou's hamster out of the cage and she couldn't find it anywhere.

'Keep looking,' encouraged Mom. 'Hamsters hide in all sorts of funny places.'

So Dipou searched all morning. She looked in her dolls' house and even got Dad to prize open a floorboard, but there were no little sounds of scuffling feet. By lunchtime she was tired, worried and hungry. 'Can I have an apple, Mom?' she asked.

'Help yourself,' said Mom.

Dipou went to the dish. There were four apples in it, and one of them looked a bit furry. Dipou looked closer. It moved. The other apples had little teethmarks in them.

'I've found my hamster!' cried Dipou with relief. 'At least he won't need any lunch!'

The Dolls' Tea-Party

Mommy Doll had spent a busy morning baking cookies. Amanda Doll popped one into her mouth. 'Yummy!' she said. Mommy Doll slapped her hand.

'Naughty,' she said. 'Wait until our tea-party!'

But Mommy Doll felt sad. All those delicious cookies and no one to eat them but greedy little Amanda and Baby Billy.

'I wish we could have a visitor,' she sighed.

She set the table and was just putting the cookies on the

table when there was a knock on the dolls' house door. Amanda ran to open it. A funny wooden man stood on the doorstep. He had a wooden hat on.

'Good afternoon,' said the little man. 'I'm Mr Noah. I live in the Ark, and I've always wanted to see inside a dolls' house. Would you mind if I came in and looked around?'

Mommy Doll smiled and opened the door wide. 'Welcome!' she said. 'I have just made lots of delicious cookies and I should be delighted if you would join us for a tea-party!'

Mr Noah is Missing

The Noah's Ark stood in the toyshop window. It was being sold cheaply because Mr Noah was missing. Nobody knew what had happened. When the owner of the shop had unpacked the Ark, Mr Noah simply wasn't there!

What no-one knew was that Mr Noah had gone visiting. In the back of the shop was an old dolls' house and Mr Noah, who had never been in a house before, had climbed out of the packing box and knocked on the dolls' house door. At the very moment when the toyshop owner was putting: 'Incomplete – 20% off original price' on the Ark, Mr Noah was sitting down for a tea party with all the Doll family!

Very soon a small girl visited the shop. 'Look, Daddy,' said Melanie. 'There's a cheap Noah's Ark for sale.'

'That's lucky,' said Melanie's father. 'I think I can just about afford it.'

The toyshop man explained that Mr Noah was missing, and started to pack the figures into a cardboard box.

'Wait for me,' puffed a little voice, though the humans didn't hear it. Mr Noah ran across the toyshop floor and jumped into the box. Just in time! The lid slammed down.

'Look, Daddy,' said Melanie later as they unpacked the Ark. 'Mr Noah isn't missing at all. He's here!'

The Glass Swan

The glass swan sat on Mrs Smith's mantel between two china dogs. It felt very unhappy. For though the dogs sat, as dogs should, guarding the mantel, the swan sat as if it were swimming – only there was no water.

One day Mrs Smith's little granddaughter, Emily, came to stay. She loved the glass swan. 'Poor Swan,' she said. 'You should be swimming on a lake. I know what I can do,' and she ran to the shops to buy something. She came back with a shiny round glass mirror. The swan had a lake at last!

Toby Jug

Toby Jug sat on a shelf in Mr Watkins' house with 20 other toby jugs. He had a jolly, smiling face, but in fact he was rather sad, for no one really noticed him. All they ever said was: 'What a magnificent collection of toby jugs you have, Mr Watkins.'

'I don't want to be a collection,' said Toby Jug. 'I want to be *me*.'

One day Mr Watkins came home with some more toby jugs.

'I haven't room for all these new ones,' he said. 'I'll have to sell one of the old ones.'

Mrs Watkins looked at the shelf. 'Don't sell that fellow, will you?' she said, pointing to Toby Jug. 'I've always liked him and he'd do nicely for my flowers.' She took him off the shelf and filled him with sweet peas. Toby Jug was thrilled. Now everybody notices him and says: 'Mr Watkins, that's the jolliest toby jug we ever have seen.'

Performing Seal, Retired

Lucy was playing ball in her yard. She threw the ball high in the air and it fell, not at her feet, but over the fence in the yard next door.

'Phooey,' said Lucy. 'I'll have to ask our new neighbors to throw it back.'

But before she could do that, the ball suddenly came sailing over the fence.

'Thank you,' called Lucy.

'Honk, honk,' came the reply. Lucy was surprised. It didn't sound like someone saying hello. In fact, it didn't sound like a person at all!

'Honk, honk,' went the voice again. Lucy fetched a ladder and looked over the fence. Whatever could it be? A dog? A pig? A boy playing tricks?

But when Lucy saw what it was, she had the shock of her life. She could never have imagined that her new neighbors would have such an exciting pet. For it wasn't a dog – it was a seal!

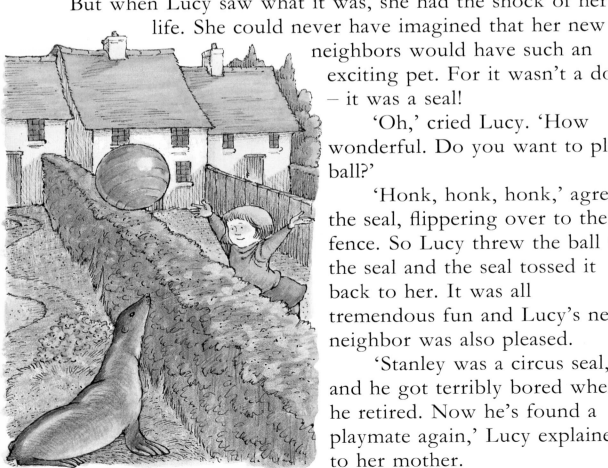

'Oh,' cried Lucy. 'How wonderful. Do you want to play ball?'

'Honk, honk, honk,' agreed the seal, flippering over to the fence. So Lucy threw the ball to the seal and the seal tossed it back to her. It was all tremendous fun and Lucy's new neighbor was also pleased.

'Stanley was a circus seal, and he got terribly bored when he retired. Now he's found a playmate again,' Lucy explained to her mother.

Cinderella

Perrault

There was once a girl called Cinderella who had two jealous step-sisters. Because the girl was so much more beautiful than either of them they kept her out of sight, working in the kitchen.

One day the step-sisters went off to the prince's Grand Ball, leaving Cinderella sitting by the hearth. After they had left, Cinderella's fairy godmother happened to call. Cinderella told her how much she'd love to go to the Ball.

'That can easily be arranged,' said her godmother, and straightaway she turned a pumpkin into a golden coach and some rats into coachmen. Cinderella was given a glittering white silk ballgown but warned to be back home by midnight.

When Cinderella arrived at the Ball the prince noticed her at once and they danced together all evening. But then the clock struck midnight and a dreadful thing happened! The coach and horses changed back into a pumpkin and rats, and Cinderella, running down the palace steps, found herself once more in rags. In her rush she dropped one of her little glass slippers. The prince picked it up, and decided to find its owner. He went round the whole kingdom, until he came to Cinderella's home. The two step-sisters each tried to force their foot into the slipper, but they couldn't. Then it was Cinderella's turn. The slipper fitted perfectly, and the prince knew he had found his own true love at last.

Judy's Island

Judy wanted to own an island. She didn't mind how small it was, so long as she could stand on it with at least one foot.

One night it rained and rained and when Judy looked out in the morning she could see lots of water everywhere. She put on her boots and ran out into the yard. The grass was a lake, and right in the middle Judy could see an island – an old upturned bucket that Mom used to put weeds in. She sploshed across the grass to it. And she could *just* stand on it – with both feet!

Judy was very happy. At last she had found her own island.

Gentleman Ladybug

Godfrey was a very smart ladybug. He had a wonderful red shiny coat and lots of black spots. He should have been happy but he wasn't.

'I'm not a *lady*bug,' he said crossly to Peter who had found Godfrey under a foxglove leaf. Peter showed Godfrey his nature book. 'But it says so here – you're exactly like the picture.'

'But I'm not a *lady*,' insisted Godfrey. 'I'm a *boy*, like you!'

Later, in the classroom, Peter pinned up a drawing on the wall. It was a very good picture of Godfrey, complete with lots of spots. But underneath the picture Peter had written in his very best handwriting: 'Godfrey the gentlemanbug'!

Party Fright

Some children are frightened of the dentist, and some don't like school. Some are afraid of big dogs, and others of fireworks. Rasheed was frightened of parties.

Rasheed was bad at games, and always lost. He thought all the other children were sneering at him.

'You mustn't be frightened of people laughing at you,' said his mother. 'Everyone's good at something.'

'I'm not,' said Rasheed, and burst into tears.

At Mandy's party they played hide-and-seek. Rasheed decided to hide somewhere so secret that no one would ever find him and then he could stay there until his mother came to collect him. Mandy had a big, fluffy comforter, and everyone had put their coats on top of it. Rasheed crawled right under the coats and right under the comforter and lay there, very still.

'Where's Rasheed?' he heard them all cry.

'I'm tired of looking,' said Mandy, sitting on her bed.

'Ouch!' cried Rasheed.

'I've found him!' shrieked Mandy. 'But that's really clever, Rasheed. No one could have guessed!'

'Everyone's good at something,' thought Rasheed. Even hiding. After that, he felt much better and was never frightened of parties again.

The Stray Dog

Mrs Moffat lived all alone in a little cottage in the forest. She wasn't lonely, or so she told herself, because she had a yard to work in, books to read and a thousand and one chores to do around the house. But sometimes, when the wind howled down the chimney and she thought she heard footsteps outside in the night, she felt just a little bit frightened.

'What you need is a dog,' said a neighbor.

'Nonsense!' said Mrs Moffat. 'Dogs are nasty, messy brutes!'

It was a long walk into the village and often Mrs Moffat wished she had someone to talk to.

'What you need is a dog,' said the butcher, wrapping up her meat.

'Nonsense!' said Mrs Moffat. 'A dog will eat me out of house and home.'

One night when the rain was lashing at the window panes Mrs Moffat heard a funny, snuffly noise on the doorstep. She opened the door, and peered out cautiously.

On the mat stood a very wet, very muddy and very thin dog. It whined and looked at her with pleading eyes.

'Come in,' said Mrs Moffat. 'But only until the rain stops. Not a moment longer.'

But once the dog was inside and Mrs Moffat had rubbed it dry, given it some supper and made it lie down in front of a roaring fire, she sighed and said to herself, 'Perhaps I *do* need a dog. Yes, I do think a dog would be a very good idea after all!'

Great-Granny's Trip

On the day before Great-Granny's 95th birthday, Tim asked her what she'd like for a present.

'What about a shawl, or a nice warm pair of slippers?' he said.

But Great-Granny shook her head. 'I don't want that sort of present,' she said. 'But I do know what I would like.' And when she whispered in Tim's ear, his eyes grew round with excitement.

'Great!' he said. 'May I come too?'

Great-Granny's birthday dawned bright and still.

'Just right for the trip,' said Dad and Mom.

Neither Great-Granny nor Tim had ever been up in a helicopter before. They could see the whole world at their feet. It was the best treat ever – for Tim as well as for Great-Granny!

The Cook and the Fairies

Traditional

There was once a woman who was a wonderful cook. She cooked so well that she was stolen away by the fairies, who wanted her to work for them. The woman was determined to escape, but she was clever, and didn't let the fairies know this. Instead, she sent them running back for her bowl, her flour, and all the things she would need to bake a cake. Then, when everything was ready, she said: 'I can't bake a cake without my little cat purring by my side.' So the fairies fetched her cat. Then the woman said: 'I can't beat the mixture properly without my dog snoring beside me.' So the fairies fetched her dog. But then the woman wanted her baby and after that, her husband.

'Now perhaps she'll get down to it,' said the exhausted fairies. And indeed, the woman started to make the cake. But the dog started to bark and the baby to scream, while her husband stood on the cat's tail so that it yowled, and yowled and yowled.

Now, there's one thing that the fairies hate and that's a lot of noise. They put their hands to their ears and drove the woman, her husband, the baby, the dog and the cat right out of fairyland and back to their own home!

Man in the Moon

The Man in the Moon was lonely. He lived so far away that no one had visited him for a very long time. Then, one day, he saw a tiny speck in the sky. It grew bigger and bigger and then 'zoom', it landed 'plonk' on the Moon.

'Ouch!' exclaimed the Man in the Moon. 'You've landed on my tummy!'

'Sorry!' said a voice, and a white-clad figure climbed out of the rocket.

'Welcome to my home,' said the Man in the Moon. 'Perhaps you'd care for some refreshment?'

'Yes, please,' said the spaceman. 'I've come a long way!'

So the Man in the Moon and the spaceman sat down to a splendid meal of green cheese and moondrops.

The Leopard and the Fox

Aesop

The leopard is a very beautiful creature, with his yellow coat and black spots. The leopard thought so too. He thought he was twice as handsome as the King of the Jungle, and was far too proud to associate with all the other animals and birds. Soon everybody was tired of his boasting.

One day a fox was passing by while the leopard was admiring himself in a pool.

'It's all very well to be handsome,' remarked the fox. 'But in the end, it's brains that count.'

For beauty, after all, is only skin deep.

The Ass and the Frogs

Aesop

One day an ass, with a huge load on his back, stumbled and fell into a bog. 'Help!' cried the ass. 'Let me out of this horrible smelly place!' And he brayed and brayed.

Some frogs, who lived in the bog, heard his loud cries and said to him: 'You've only been in the bog for a few minutes, why are you making such a fuss? How would you feel if you'd been here as long as we have?'

Which goes to show that only familiarity makes things acceptable to us.

The Bees, the Drones and the Wasp

Aesop

The bees and the drones were arguing about who had made the honeycomb, deep in the hollow tree. The quarrel became so serious that they decided to take the case to Judge Wasp.

The Judge thought about the problem very carefully, for he had a difficult task before him. Both the bees and the drones looked very similar, and it was therefore impossible to decide who were the rightful owners of the honeycomb.

Then the Judge made a decision. He asked the bees and drones each to build a hive. 'I can then tell who owns the honeycomb by the shape of the cells and the taste of the honey.'

The bees agreed immediately, but the drones refused.

'It's very clear to me,' said Judge Wasp, 'that the bees built the honeycomb, and I declare them the rightful owners.'

The drones all flew away, and made it their business never to show themselves before the wise Judge again.

So, always judge a person by his actions, rather than his words.

The Magical Birthday Cake

It was John's birthday and his mother had asked a magician to his party. At first, the magician did all the usual tricks: rabbits appeared out of top-hats, and coins from behind children's ears. But John, who was very spoiled, soon became bored.

'That's easy,' he scoffed. 'I bet you can't do *real* magic.'

'Try me,' said the magician, annoyed.

'I bet you can't make my birthday cake grow as big as a house,' said John, who was also very greedy.

The magician waved his wand, and suddenly, the birthday cake began to grow and grow. Very soon it was as big as the table. But still it grew. It flattened all the cookies and sandwiches. It made the table tilt over. John was very frightened.

'Stop it!' he yelled. 'At once!'

Now, there were two things the magician didn't like. One was spoiled and greedy little boys. The other was being bossed around. So he swirled his wand and the cake stopped growing and started to shrink instead. It grew smaller and smaller, until it was no bigger than a marble.

'Stop!' wailed John, but it was too late. The birthday cake had shrunk into nothing at all. All its lovely, creamy topping, its seven candles and its marzipan railway engine had disappeared completely.

'You really *are* a magician,' breathed the other children, as the magician swept from the room.

34

The Mystery Pet

Dean's puppy needed an injection, so Dean took it to the vet. There were lots of other people there holding cats in baskets and dogs on leashes. Dean's puppy skidded on the floor with excitement – there were so many other dogs to play with!

Suddenly the door opened and a woman came in, carrying a big cardboard box. Dean stared at it. What sort of pet could it be? It didn't bark, it didn't miaow, it didn't even scuffle.

'Excuse me,' she said, 'is the special vet on duty? The one who knows all about exotic pets?'

'Exotic pets!' thought Dean. 'It must be a whopper, given the size of the box!' But even Dean was shocked by the woman's next words.

'It's my python,' explained the lady. 'It has toothache.'

St George's Son

St George was very famous for fighting a dragon. But have you ever heard of Magnus, St George's son?

Magnus was a soft-hearted little boy, and when he heard what St George had done, he burst into tears.

'The poor dragon,' he sobbed. 'And what about Mommy dragon and all the baby dragons waiting at home?'

'I killed Mommy dragon on the way back,' said St George carelessly. 'And there was only one baby. I saw it scuttling away.'

'Then it's an orphan,' cried Magnus.

That night, Magnus couldn't sleep. He kept thinking of the baby dragon. More than anything in the world he wanted the baby dragon for a pet.

So when the Moon was bright, Magnus put on a warm cloak and set off across the plain to find the little dragon. After a while, he came to a rock. Behind the rock was a faint glow and Magnus could hear a sort of squealing noise.

'I've come to rescue you, little dragon,' said Magnus. 'You can live in the cellar and eat coal and when you're older I can fly on your back to the stars.'

And very gently, Magnus, son of brave St George the dragon killer, folded his warm cloak around the little dragon and carried it home.

The Prize Sunflowers

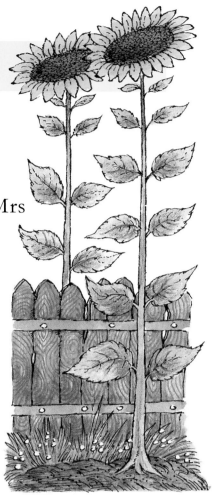

Mrs Potts and Mrs Winters were neighbors. They were the best of friends – until the day they both entered the competition to grow the biggest sunflower in the village. On that day, Mrs Potts and Mrs Winters became deadly enemies.

Each day, both ladies boasted about who had the best sunflower.

Then one night there was a big storm. In the morning both sunflowers lay flat on their faces.

'We'd better pick them,' said Mrs Potts. 'Would you like them?'

And they were the best of friends once more.

Old Cat's Excursion

Mrs Partridge was getting ready for the Old People's Excursion. Her cat, Dorcas, watched her put on her pale blue coat and best hat. 'Why can't I go too?' wondered Dorcas. 'I'm an old cat.' So when the bus drew up at the gate and Mrs Partridge climbed aboard, Dorcas slipped on to the bus and crouched under the back seat. Nobody saw her. When the bus stopped at the seaside, everybody got out. But nobody saw Dorcas trotting down to the sea and flicking her paw in the water. Nor did they see her steal some crab from the fish booth. And they certainly didn't see her climb back on the bus and curl up under Mrs Partridge's coat.

'What a purr-fect day,' purred Dorcas, sleepily.

Camping

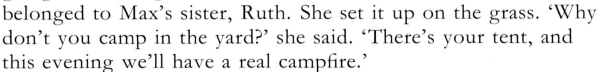

Max was fed up. He had had measles which meant he couldn't go camping. So he moped round the house, getting under Mom's feet.

'It's not fair,' he said. 'I feel lots better.'

Mom had an idea. She went into the garage and brought out an old tent that had belonged to Max's sister, Ruth. She set it up on the grass. 'Why don't you camp in the yard?' she said. 'There's your tent, and this evening we'll have a real campfire.'

Later, Mom and Dad fixed up the barbecue on the patio. Then along came Aunt Meg, Uncle David, and Max's cousins, Harry and John.

They cooked hot dogs and baked potatoes and hamburgers, and after supper Dad got out his guitar and everyone sang campfire songs. Then Max, Harry and John took their sleeping bags into the tent and listened to the grown-ups talking until the Moon came up.

The Two Fir Trees

There were once two fir trees growing in a forest. One was tall and stately, the other short and sturdy.

'How elegant I'll look this Christmas, covered in tinsel and lights!' boasted the tall tree.

The little fir tree felt sad. No one would want her. She was too short and bushy.

Soon the woodcutters came and cut down the big tree. The little tree shuddered when she heard the sound of the axe.

'It would be best to dig up this little one, not cut it,' said the woodcutter.

So the little fir tree was dug up and planted in a green pot. That Christmas she found herself sitting on a window-sill, decked out with tinsel.

After Christmas, she was planted in the yard, where she soon started to grow.

The little fir tree never knew what became of the tall tree, but she grew more graceful every year and was always dug up for Christmas.

The Incredible Egg

'What did your dad bring you back from vacation?' asked Mark.

'A great big pretend egg made from wood,' said Sandy proudly. 'It's as big as a football and so strong you can stand on it. Let's paint it, shall we?'

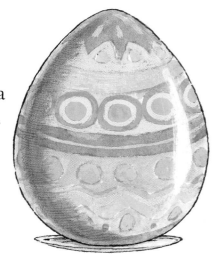

When the two boys had finished, the egg looked exotic and strange like a wonderful Easter Egg.

'Incredible!' said Mark.

Four Friends and the Robbers

Grimm

Once upon a time there were four animals – a donkey, a dog, a cat and a cockerel. They had all been ill-treated by their owners and one day they set off to find a new life for themselves.

By and by they came to an old cottage in the woods.

'Here's a good home for us,' said the dog. But when the donkey peered in, he saw a gang of robbers, surrounded by their stolen treasures. 'We must stop them!' he said and the four friends made a wonderful plan for scaring the robbers away.

The dog jumped on the donkey's back, the cat on the dog's, and the cockerel on top of the cat. Then all four brayed and barked and miaowed and crowed. The robbers sprang to their feet and saw a terrifying shape at the moonlit window.

'Help! A monster!' they cried, and they fled into the forest.

Then the donkey, the dog, the cat and the cockerel ran into the cottage and had the feast of their lives on the robbers' supper. And the four animals lived happily in the little cottage for the rest of their lives.

News Day

'Tomorrow is News Day,' said Mrs Barton. 'I want all of you to come in with a piece of exciting news to tell the class.'

Debbie worried about News Day all evening. Nothing exciting ever happened to her. She hadn't been given a pony for her birthday and spacemen hadn't landed in the yard. Nor had any robbers held up the bank on Main Street. Debbie walked slowly to school the next morning, still worrying.

'Help!' somebody suddenly cried. 'I'm stuck!'

Debbie looked up. It was Kevin Powell, clinging, terrified, to one of the branches of the oak tree. He was very high up and looked as though he would fall at any moment.

'Get my Mom or Dad!' called Kevin. 'They'll help me.'

Debbie ran up the street and banged on the Powells' door.

'Silly boy,' said Mr Powell, and took a ladder from the shed. By now a crowd had gathered by the tree. Kevin's dad leaned the ladder against the tree and climbed up until he reached the boy. Then he slowly brought him down to safety. Kevin grinned at Debbie. 'Thanks for saving me,' he said.

Debbie was late for school. 'Sorry I'm late, Mrs Barton,' she said. 'But something very exciting happened on the way here!'

41

The Missing Earring

It was Christmas morning and Mom was looking everywhere for one of her pearl earrings. 'I had it a few weeks ago,' she said. 'Wherever can it be? Perhaps I should have asked for a new pair as a present.' She was joking, but she was also upset. They were her best earrings.

Christmas dinner was wonderful with turkey and stuffing and a special cake called Christmas pudding.

'There are six silver coins in the Christmas pudding,' said Mom. 'So don't swallow them.'

'I've found a coin,' cried Michael, 'and your pearl earring!'

'Thank you,' laughed Mom. 'I must have stirred it into the batter.'

Cindy's Treat

It was Christmas Eve and Cindy Spaniel could smell something good. Her nose took her out of the kitchen and into the hall where the Christmas tree stood. Underneath it were four boxes of candy. Cindy had a *very* good nose for candy. It was her favorite treat. She ate it all – chocolates, candy canes and mints. Afterwards, she felt just a little bit sick.

On Christmas morning the children gave Cindy a special bone-shaped parcel. By now Cindy was feeling very sick indeed. Mom came into the bedroom, really mad. 'I thought so,' she said when she saw Cindy's unhappy face. 'Candy is for people, *bones* are for dogs.'

Cindy agreed, until she felt better. And then – she ate her bone!

The Princess and the Pea

Andersen

There was once a prince who would only marry a real princess. There were many princesses around, but none of them delicate or sensitive enough for the prince's tastes. Then one day a princess came to stay. She was as fair as the fairest flower. She could sing, she could dance, and her laughter was like silver bells.

'But is she a *real* princess?' the prince asked his mother.

That night the queen led the princess to the best bedchamber in the palace. She ordered 20 mattresses to be placed on the bed, and on top of them 20 feather eiderdowns. The princess lay on top of all of these and covered herself with silk sheets and the softest woven blankets.

Next morning the queen asked her guest how she had slept.

'I'm sorry to say I didn't sleep a wink,' she said. 'There was something very hard under the mattress.'

Then the queen knew she had found a bride for her son, for she had placed a pea under the bottom mattress, and only a real princess would have been delicate and sensitive enough to feel it.

Goldilocks and the Three Bears

Southey

There once was a nosy little girl called Goldilocks. One day she found a cottage in the woods, and because it was empty and she really was very nosy, she decided to go in.

Inside she found three bowls of porridge on the table. She tasted the first, but it was too hot. She tasted the second, but it was too cold. She tasted the third and it was just right, so she ate it all.

There were three chairs round the table. She sat on one, but it was too high. She sat on the second, but it was too wide. So she sat on the third, and it broke into little pieces.

'I think I'll take a rest,' said Goldilocks, and she went upstairs to bed. The first bed was too hard, the second too soft, but the smallest was just right, and she fell asleep on it.

Just then the bears who owned the cottage returned. Father and Mother Bear were shocked and the littlest bear cried, 'Someone's eaten *all* my porridge. And that someone has *broken* my chair!' The bears went upstairs and found Goldilocks fast asleep on the littlest bear's bed. She woke up and was so frightened that she ran home and was never, ever nosy again.

The Peacock and the Rooster

The peacock and the rooster were strutting in the farmyard.

'My tail is longer than yours,' said the peacock.

'Mine has fine blue and green feathers,' said the rooster.

But the peacock was not impressed. 'Not only has mine got blue and green feathers,' he said, 'but it has eyes, too!'

The farmyard was very muddy, and the peacock didn't notice that his tail was trailing on the ground.

'Ha!' crowed the rooster. 'More like brown, I'd say!'

For the peacock's tail was covered in mud. But the rooster's short and colorful tail gleamed bright in the sun.

Hilda Hen's Easter Eggs

Hilda Hen was very proud of herself. She had laid four beautiful brown eggs for the Dobbin family's breakfast. Now she was watching Mark Dobbin searching for something in the garden.

'Hilda Hen!' he called. 'Look what I've got!' Hilda Hen looked. In Mark's basket were four brightly colored egg-shaped objects. One was red with silver spots, one was yellow with green stars, one was pink and blue and one was orange and purple.

'They're *your* eggs,' said Mark. 'We painted them for Easter and Dad laid a treasure hunt for me.'

'Well I never!' said Hilda Hen.

Mouse Trouble

The mouse trouble started when Vicky bought two white mice. She kept them in a cage in the attic because her cat, Barney, loved chasing mice and catching them, if possible.

The trouble was that Vicky's mice were not the only ones in the house. That night, when the family had all gone to bed, two pairs of beady eyes peered out into the dark attic from a mousehole.

'Psst, Margie, there are some *white mice* out there in a cage,' whispered Max Mouse.

Margie immediately felt sorry for the little prisoners. 'We must let them out at once,' she said. She ran to the cage and nibbled at the wooden catch until the mice were free.

'You'll have to find your own hole,' Max explained. 'But don't go downstairs, there's a ca – '

Too late! The two white mice had already squeezed under the attic door and fled downstairs.

Barney was sleeping on Vicky's bed when the two white mice rushed in and ran up his back. Barney leaped up and chased the mice. Terrified, they sped back into the attic and crouched in their cage until Barney had gone.

'It's much nicer in the cage,' they both agreed.

Page Girl

Susan, Becky's sister, was getting married and Becky was going to be her bridesmaid. Susan wanted her to wear a blue frilly dress with yellow buttercups and carry a posy.

But when Susan had shown Becky a picture of the bridesmaid's dress, Becky had hated it. She didn't like wearing dresses, especially frilly ones.

Mom and Susan could see that Becky was going to be difficult. 'But what can we *do*?' asked Susan. 'I don't want an unhappy bridesmaid.'

Susan's fiancé, Brian, was in the navy and he was going to wear his uniform. 'Pity there aren't any little boys in the family,' he joked. 'Then we could have had a page-boy in a sailor suit.'

Suddenly Susan had an idea.

The wedding day arrived at last. Susan looked beautiful in a long cream dress with a lace train. Brian looked very handsome in his naval uniform. And Becky, following behind, was the very smartest of all – in her sailor suit and bell-bottom trousers!

The Tortoise's Home

'Why is it that everyone has a home but me?' complained Tortoise to Mouse. He had just visited his friend, Rabbit, in his cosy burrow. 'Robin has a snug little nest in an old kettle and Horse has a wonderful stable with a wooden door. Even Pig lives in a sty, although it is a bit on the messy side.'

'But you *have* got a home,' said Mouse. 'It's a very nice home, too. You can carry it around with you and you don't get wet when you're caught in the rain.'

'Of course!' said Tortoise. 'My home is on my back!'

The Monster at the Window

Beth liked her new home. It had a long yard with a swing, a spooky cellar and an attic. Above all, Beth liked her little bedroom with the sloping roof. She arranged all her glass animals on the window-sill.

The first night, Beth climbed into her bed with the yellow-flowered comforter. Mom drew the yellow curtains, then turned off the light, and Beth heard her creak-creaking down the stairs.

Suddenly Beth felt very lonely. 'Don't go,' she pleaded, but Mom didn't hear.

Everything was in the wrong place. The dresser was where the closet used to be, and the chair was by the window instead of behind the door. There were strange, humpy things on top of the dresser. Beth shivered. What could they be?

Then Beth heard a tap-tapping at the window. 'It's a monster!' she thought. She dived under the comforter so she couldn't hear it. Perhaps if the monster couldn't see her it would go away.

When she woke in the morning she could see that the humpy things were the books she hadn't unpacked. And tap-tapping against the window pane was a beautiful flowering cherry tree.

'A cherry tree! A friend! Not a monster at all,' thought Beth.

The Witch's Dog

'I want a black dog,' said the little old lady firmly.

The owner of Barkwell Dogs' Home took her along a row of cages containing dogs of all descriptions.

'There's this jolly little fellow,' he said.

'But he's got a white chin,' complained the little old lady. Then she saw exactly the one she was looking for – a small, neat, obedient and completely black dog.

'That's the one I want!' she cried.

The little black dog trotted out of the Home behind his new mistress. The owner watched them go, but he could not guess what she was saying.

'The first thing you will have to learn,' said the little old lady, putting on her pointed hat, 'is how to ride on a broomstick.'

And off they both went, over the rooftops.

49

Jigsaw Puzzle

Karen had been given an enormous jigsaw puzzle of a castle for her birthday. She was very excited and she could not wait to get started. But the jigsaw was very complicated. It had a moat, a keep and a drawbridge. It took Karen three days to do, and on the third day she found there were some pieces missing. The people standing by the moat couldn't enter the castle because there was no drawbridge.

Karen searched everywhere. Finally, she found the missing pieces under the table. She clicked them into place. 'Mom!' she cried, 'I've finished!'

Mom came to admire the puzzle, and Karen gave a gasp of surprise. 'All those people by the moat,' she said. 'They aren't there any more! They must have crossed the drawbridge and gone into the castle!'

Stacey's Christening

Darren's baby sister, Stacey, was going to be christened. His big cousin, Joan, was one of the godmothers. He liked Joan. She was *his* godmother as well, and gave him terrific presents.

But he was fed up about the christening. Everyone was cooing and aahing over Stacey and saying all sorts of mushy things about her. She had even been given presents, presents that Darren knew she was too young to enjoy. He felt very left out.

Then Mom told him to dress in his gray flannel suit. He hated his suit and pulled the tie around so it didn't look so dumb. He stomped off down the road to the church between Gran and Grandad.

'The little lamb!' cooed Great Aunt Ethel, peering at Stacey. 'Isn't she *good*!' At this, Stacey opened her mouth and roared and roared.

Darren put his hands to his ears. 'Stupid Great Aunt Ethel,' he thought. 'She's really set her off!'

When they had reached the font, Stacey was still roaring. The vicar couldn't hear himself speak.

'Can't *anyone* stop that baby crying?' asked Grandad.

Darren stepped forward. 'I can,' he said, and he tickled Stacey's chin and made his ugly monster face.

Stacey stopped crying and started to chuckle instead.

'The little lamb,' cooed Great Aunt Ethel again.

But Gran smiled at Darren. 'Thank you,' she said.

Top Chef

Mom asked Gary to help her do some cooking.

'Cooking's stupid!' said Gary. 'Cooking's for girls.'

'Some of the best cooks are men,' said Mom, 'and I want you to help me make some special cookies.'

Mom sifted flour and added some sugar and ginger. 'Mix butter into the mixture, stir in some molasses and make a sticky ball,' she told Gary. Then Mom rolled it flat and cut it into shapes.

'Wow!' said Gary. 'They *are* special cookies.'

Between them Mom and Gary cut out 12 shapes and baked them in the oven. And out came – 12 gingerbread boys!

'I think I'll be a chef when I grow up,' said Gary, as he ate his third gingerbread man. 'Because I did like making these special cookies.'

Rainbow Playground

One night a big storm completely destroyed the goblins' playground. When Grendel, Griselda and Gareth went out to play the next morning, they found their merry-go-round had been smashed to pieces and their swings blown away.

'What shall we do?' wailed Gareth. 'It will take months to build another one.'

Just then the sun came out – and with it the most beautiful rainbow.

'Are you thinking what I'm thinking?' said Griselda.

'Yippee!' said the three goblins. They clambered up the rainbow and slid all the way down the other side!

Prince Jolly-Roger

Prince Jolly-Roger was a royal prince who sailed the seven seas with a parrot called Perkins and a ship's cat named Monty.

One day Prince Jolly-Roger discovered a secret island. It was very beautiful with beaches of silvery sand, turquoise-blue tide pools and lush green palm trees. Monty curled up in a nice shady spot under a date palm and Perkins perched on top of a tall coconut tree.

'Now I must dig for treasure,' said Prince Jolly-Roger, who knew this was the sort of thing pirates did on desert islands. He took a spade from the ship, but then wondered where to start.

'It's a pity I haven't got a treasure map,' he thought.

Then he saw that Monty had woken up. He was digging a very neat hole in the sand. Something gold could be seen glinting in the hole.

'You clever cat!' said Prince Jolly-Roger. 'I do believe you've struck treasure.'

Prince Jolly-Roger dug deeper. He found a golden crown, studded with emeralds. Prince Jolly-Roger put it on his head.

'Long live the King,' cried Perkins.

And so it was that King Jolly-Roger ruled over his very own island, with his two loyal subjects – Perkins the parrot and Monty the cat.

Oasis in the Desert

Kamil the Camel was feeling hot and thirsty. He had been trekking across the desert for ages. Suddenly, he became very excited. For there, far away in the distance, he could see a lovely pool surrounded by palm trees, and other camels bending to drink.

'Hmmph! An oasis!' he cried.

But his master, Ahmed, shook his head. 'No, Kamil. That's only a mirage – a reflection in the sand. There's no water there at all.' Kamil sniffed the air. Ahmed was right. He couldn't smell any water.

On and on they plodded until, at last, Kamil really could smell water. He could see exactly the same scene as he'd spotted earlier, but this time there really was an oasis and Kamil had a long, cool drink!

Old and New

Dad had bought a very old-fashioned wind-up phonograph in a junk store. There were even some records to go with it.

'I remember those tunes,' said Grandma dreamily, as Gail wound it up. 'My, *that* takes me back!' And Grandma started waltzing round the living-room.

'Teach me to waltz, Grandma,' begged Gail, and Grandma did – *one* two three, *one* two three.

'Disco-dancing,' said Grandma, 'isn't *real* dancing.'

'But it's fun, Grandma,' said Gail, and she fetched her cassette player. 'I'll show you.'

'Not like the old times,' grumbled Grandma. But soon her feet were tapping to the beat, and she started jogging around and twisting.

'Brilliant, Grandma!' laughed Gail.

Katie the Kangaroo

Katie the Kangaroo was lonely. Her son, Joey, had left her pouch two days ago, and she missed him very much. Now he was able to look after himself.

Katie hopped round the safari park and chatted to the giraffes and elephants. But she still felt lonely. 'There's nothing like having someone in your pouch!' she sighed.

Beyond the safari park lay a field, and in that field were some sheep with their families. Katie knew them well.

'Katie Kangaroo!' said Prudence Sheep. 'Just the animal! My little lamb, Bobby, gets bored so easily that I was wondering – well, whether you could take him for a trip round the safari park?'

Katie was delighted and from then on she was never lonely again, for she took little Bobby Lamb on a trip in her pouch every single day.

Glow-Worm Lights

 **G**rendel Goblin was preparing for Christmas. He had made a splendid holly wreath which he hung on his front door, and his kitchen was filled with all sorts of wonderful spicy smells as he stirred the pumpkin pie filling, and baked batches of Christmas cookies. But Grendel still wasn't satisfied.

'What I'd really like is a Christmas tree,' he said to himself. So he went into the forest and spotted a nice little Christmas tree. It was neither too small nor too large, and his gold and silver pine cones would look very good on it.

'But a Christmas tree's no good without lights, and I don't have any,' wailed Grendel.

'Excuse me,' whispered a little voice. 'Perhaps we can help you – and you can help us.'

Grendel looked down at his feet and saw a tiny glow-worm, shivering with the cold.

'We don't like the winter,' said the glow-worm. 'If you take us into your nice warm cottage, we could hang on your tree and light it for you.'

'What a splendid idea!' said Grendel.

And so the glow-worm, together with lots of his friends and relations, followed Grendel as he carried the Christmas tree home.

That Christmas, Grendel's Christmas tree, shining with soft glow-worm lights and covered with silver and gold pine cones, was quite the most beautiful in the whole of Goblin Town.

The Emperor's New Clothes

Andersen

There was once a very vain emperor who loved new clothes more than anything else in the world. One day, two tailors appeared at the palace. They promised to make him a suit so fine that only the cleverest people would be able to see it. The emperor was delighted and watched the two tailors as they stitched away – but he couldn't see any cloth or any thread.

'If I say I can't see anything, everyone will think I'm stupid,' thought the emperor, so he held his tongue. The Chancellor and the courtiers didn't want to be thought stupid either, so when they saw – or rather, didn't see – the suit, they clapped their hands and cried: 'What a magnificent suit! Such wonderful colors! Such fine embroidery!'

The emperor decided to wear his new suit at his birthday parade. Crowds of people turned up to see him, but as they had already heard all about the invisible suit, they too pretended they could see it.

Only one small boy in the whole city hadn't heard about the suit, and he cried out: 'But the emperor hasn't any clothes on!'

And after this, all the emperor's subjects roared with laughter and cried: 'He's right! The emperor hasn't any clothes on!'

As for the two 'tailors', they sped as fast as they could out of the city and were never seen again.

The Sleeping Beauty

Perrault

Once there was a king and queen whose little daughter was going to be christened. The queen chose seven fairy godmothers for the child, who all promised her health, wealth and beauty. Alas, the king and queen forgot to invite one bad fairy. In her spite at not being invited to the christening, the bad fairy said that the princess would prick her finger and fall asleep for a hundred years.

The king and queen immediately banned all sharp needles from the kingdom. But somehow one was missed, and when the princess reached her 18th birthday, she found it and pricked her finger. She fell asleep at once, and the entire palace with her.

Time passed, and tales of the sleeping princess were told to princes in other lands. Many searched for the palace, but it had become so overgrown with trees and thorn bushes that none of them succeeded.

Then, just one hundred years after the princess had fallen asleep, a handsome young prince stumbled across the forest. He hacked his way through the trees and thorns until he reached the cobweb-covered palace and all its sleeping inhabitants. He entered and soon found the princess, asleep on her bed. He thought she was beautiful and kissed her. She awoke and fell in love with the prince straight away. Then everyone woke up. The prince and princess were married, and they all lived happily ever after.

The Missing Triangle

Sunita was going to play a triangle in the school orchestra. She was very proud of the little tune it made when all the other instruments were silent. But on the day of the concert she couldn't find her triangle, even though she ran all over the house looking for it.

'I must have it,' she wailed. 'The whole tune will be ruined without it.'

Then, suddenly, she heard a faint tinkling sound coming from the hall closet. She opened it – and there was her little brother, Prabir, playing her triangle.

'Pretty tune,' he said, and grinned impishly.

Sunita couldn't be mad. He looked so funny. 'When I come back from the concert I'll teach you to play properly,' she promised.

Prabir was delighted. And at the next concert, they both played the triangle.

The Dog and the Cock

Aesop

A dog and a cock were walking through a wood when night fell. The cock decided to go to roost in a tree, while the dog slept at its foot. But a fox saw the cock and thought he would make a good supper.

So when dawn broke and the cock crowed, the fox congratulated him on his fine voice. 'But come down so that I can hear it better,' said the sly fox.

'Certainly,' said the cock, who could see through the fox's wicked plan. 'But first you must ask my friend's permission – he's sitting at the foot of the tree over there.'

Of course when the dog saw the fox he chased him away immediately, and the two friends continued their journey in peace and safety.

The Tortoise and the Eagle

Aesop

There was once a tortoise who was very dissatisfied with the way he lived. He longed to learn how to fly and spent hours watching the birds circling in the sky. 'If only I could fly like a bird,' he sighed. 'I'm sure that if I was up there, I'd be as good as any of them.'

The more he thought about it, the more discontent he became. Then, one day, the tortoise saw an eagle flying by, and he suddenly had a very good idea.

'Please take me up into the sky with you,' pleaded the tortoise. 'If you teach me to fly, I'll reward you with anything you ask for.'

The eagle thought the tortoise was very foolish. He knew it would be an impossible task, but the tortoise went on and on, so much that the eagle finally agreed. He picked up the tortoise in his beak and flew him high into the air.

'Is this high enough for you?' asked the eagle.

'Oh, yes,' said the tortoise. 'I'll soon show all those silly ground creatures a thing or two.'

Then the eagle loosened his hold, and the poor tortoise discovered he couldn't fly at all. But it was too late. Down and down he fell until he dropped onto a big rock. He cracked his shell and bruised himself so badly that it took him weeks to recover.

Don't try for the impossible, or you may get badly hurt.

Goblin Globe-Trotter

'**I**'m going round the world,' announced Gerry Goblin.

He packed his spare tunic, a freshly-baked blueberry pie and a bottle of elderberry wine in a red-spotted handkerchief.

'Little goblins shouldn't be out after dark,' said Father Goblin, 'so be home by sunset.'

Gerry Goblin set off. He reached the edge of Peppercorn Woods, but deep inside the trees looked very dark and mysterious.

'I think I'll walk round the edge,' said Gerry to himself. And so he did, round and round until his little legs ached. He saw the edge of Goblin Village and Humple-Dumple Mountain. He saw Cockleshell Bay where he and Griselda had once spent a day. In the distance, he saw a big green swamp which was the beginning of Dragon Country.

Just as the sun was setting behind Humple-Dumple Mountain Gerry arrived back at the very same spot from which he'd started.

'How was the world?' asked Father Goblin.

'*Very* large and very tiring,' yawned Gerry. 'But one day I'm going back 'cos I want to go somewhere *really* dangerous, beyond the green swamp.'

Mother Goblin tucked him into bed. 'One day,' she said. 'When you're a big, brave goblin. But not just yet.'

And Gerry Goblin thought she might be right!

Rabbit Moves Home

Rabbit lived in a burrow underneath a big field of grain. He loved his home and was very fond of playing hide-and-seek among the stalks with all the other rabbits.

One day, Rabbit heard a lot of noise and commotion. He crouched in his burrow, terrified, and when all was quiet he poked his head out into the field. There, a terrible sight met his eyes. The grain had been cut down. His playground had disappeared. All that was left was blackened stubble.

'Well, it's no use moping,' said Rabbit. He scuttled quickly across the stubble, and what do you think he found? A lovely large wood with twisty tree roots and hidden glades – and lots of empty rabbit burrows in which to make a new home.

'Much better than a field,' said Rabbit happily.

Christmas-Tree Bird

The blue Christmas-tree bird was very beautiful. Its tail was made from white spun-glass and for years it had hung just beneath the Christmas-tree fairy from the topmost branch of the tree. But this year there were some new decorations – a frosted purple glass ball with stars, and a silver owl.

'Let's put the owl on the top branch,' said Tamsin. Poor Christmas-tree bird! He found himself stuck at the back of the tree, right against the wall.

But that night, disaster struck. The cat came into the room and pulled the owl off the tree, breaking its top. The owl could only perch in the tub. So Tamsin put the Christmas-tree bird back in its old place for everyone to admire.

Worm Watching

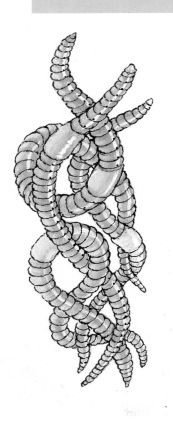

Matthew loved worms. He liked them because they were slimy and slithery. In fact, he liked them so much that he decided to start a wormery. He fetched a huge jar from the shed and filled it with dirt. Then he put four of the largest worms he could find into the jar.

'Ugh!' said Mom and Dad. 'How can you like worms?' But Matthew did. But though he watched the jar all day, he never saw his worms. They stayed deep in the middle of the earth.

One morning, Dad and Mom said, 'Why don't you watch birds? They're much more interesting.'

And so they were.

The Greedy King

Once upon a time, there was a very greedy king who loved eating cream puffs. He ate them for breakfast, lunch and tea – even dinner! In fact he ate so many that all the bakeries ran out of pastry and the dairies out of cream.

So the greedy king ordered that every store in the land become a bakery or a dairy. There were to be no more grocery stores, no hardware stores, and no clothes stores. You can imagine how dreadfully inconvenient it all was!

Very soon the king grew so fat that he started bulging out of his clothes – but because there were no clothes stores, he couldn't buy any new ones. Then one day he sat on his throne, and 'crunch!' it collapsed under his weight. But there were no furniture stores, so he couldn't have it mended.

'You must go on a diet,' said the doctor. 'And eat fresh fruit every day.' But of course there were no grocery stores. The king began to realize how foolish he had been. He called back all the storekeepers, and told them to start their businesses again.

And after that, the king only allowed himself one cream puff a day, which he ate for desert after supper!

The Girl from the Sea

Traditional

Once there was a man who fell in love with a strange and beautiful girl. He had first set eyes on her one morning while she was dancing on the sands. But the girl was one of the Seal People and when he went to speak to her, she fled, put on her seal-skin, and swam out to sea.

Now the man knew that if he stole her seal-skin, the girl could never become a seal again and would be his for ever. So the next time she was by the shore he snatched the skin away and hid it in his cottage. Then he went back for the girl, and as she was sad and lonely and frightened, she agreed to marry him.

But the girl was never really happy, for she pined for her life in the sea and for all her friends and companions. One day, while her husband was out, the girl searched the cottage for her seal-skin and finally found it deep in the cellar. She ran down to the shore with it and as she put it on, she forgot about her human husband and her life in the cottage. She swam far, far away and the man never saw her again.

The man was very sad, but sometimes, far out in the bay, he thought he could hear the sound of her voice, singing with the seals.

The Music Box

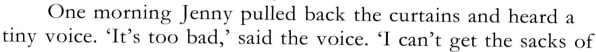

Jenny had a very unusual music box. It was shaped like a windmill and there was even a little wooden miller outside it with two sacks of grain. When Jenny turned a key the sails went round, the music played, and the little man bent down to pick up the sacks.

One day the key broke, and the windmill's sails stopped turning round.

'I'll get it fixed,' said Jenny, but she forgot. The little windmill stood, neglected and dusty, on Jenny's window-sill.

One morning Jenny pulled back the curtains and heard a tiny voice. 'It's too bad,' said the voice. 'I can't get the sacks of grain into the mill. And even if I could, the sails can't turn, so the grain won't be ground.'

Jenny bent down to look at the little miller. His two sacks had cobwebs on them. 'I'm so sorry,' she said humbly. 'I'll get a new key this very morning.'

And she did. She rushed back with the key, and turned it in the music box. The pretty tune tinkled out, the little miller set to work again, as the sails of the windmill turned round.

Pinchy Shoes

Jane had a pair of red leather shoes with little straps on them. She loved them and she wore them every day to school, and every weekend when she went shopping with Mom.

One day Mom realized that Jane was limping. 'What's the matter?' she asked.

'Nothing,' said Jane, who didn't want to admit that her shoes were pinching. But her shoes felt worse and worse every day and Mom soon noticed. 'Your shoes are too small,' she said. 'You need some new ones.'

Jane was very upset. She didn't want new shoes. She loved her old ones. So she sulked around the stores with Mom as they looked for another suitable pair. Then Mom found another pair of red ones, with bows instead of straps.

'Very smart,' she said.

'Mmm,' said Jane, still unsure. But she was soon skipping down the street.

Goblin Fishing

It was a lovely sunny day and Gareth Goblin decided to go fishing at Collywobble Lake. He wanted Griselda to go with him, too, but Griselda didn't like fishing very much as she always felt sorry for the poor fish. But she put on her sun-hat, picked up her swim suit and trotted along beside Gareth with all his fishing gear.

When they arrived at the lake, Griselda put on her swim suit. 'You can fish if you like,' she said. 'But I'm going swimming.'

At the end of the day, what do you think Gareth had caught? One old boot, a stick, a flat stone, and a rubber ring. And do you know why? Griselda had frightened all the fish away from the bait, and tied those things on to Gareth's fishing line instead!

Dog Show

Tracey had entered her dog, Muffet, in the local dog show. Her brother, Leigh, was very scornful. 'Who'd give a prize to that old scruff?' he mocked. 'He's all hair and legs.'

It was true. Poor Muffet was a shaggy, long-legged mongrel and was neither beautiful nor obedient.

All the same, Tracey combed his ears and brushed his coat until it shone. She even dusted him with talcum powder to improve his smell. Finally, they set off to the show.

First, there was the prize for the most handsome dog. (Muffet didn't win that). Next, there was the prize for the most obedient dog. (Muffet didn't win that, either). Then, there was the prize for the fastest dog. Each dog had to run after a ball and bring it back to its owner.

'You might win that,' said Tracey hopefully. 'Your legs are long enough.' But there was a greyhound there, too, and greyhounds are very fast.

As soon as the contest began, the greyhound shot off at top speed. But he ran so fast that he rushed straight past the ball and had to go back for it.

But Muffet's favorite game was retrieving balls and Tracey had played it with him many times. Muffet ran straight to the ball, and then ran back with it, dropping it at Tracey's feet.

'Brilliant!' said the judge, handing Tracey the prize.

Play Horse

Andy was fed up. He had been chosen to be the back end of a horse in the annual school play.

'Why couldn't I be the wicked wizard,' he complained, 'or the handsome prince? Nobody sees the back end of a horse!'

All through the rehearsals Andy fooled around. He started going backward and kicking his legs out in a skittish way.

'Behave, Andy!' snapped Mrs Barton. But Andy was enjoying himself too much. He thought he'd get a good laugh on the night of the play.

The opening night arrived. Rows and rows of parents were there to watch. Andy clattered on to the stage with his front half, Darren.

'Now,' thought Andy. 'I'll really steal the show.' He kicked up his right leg and wiggled it. Then he started walking backward.

'Stop it!' hissed Darren. 'You'll split the horse!'

Too late! Andy parted from Darren, and 'crash!' He'd fallen off the stage into the front row. Everyone roared with laughter.

Andy was furious.

'Well, you wanted to steal the show,' said Mrs Barton.

The Big Jam Sandwich

There was once a giant called James. He looked terrifying, but in fact he was very gentle. Although he looked as if he'd eat a whole regiment of soldiers for his dinner, he was really a vegetarian – and that means he didn't eat meat. Nevertheless, when James walked toward the town, everyone else ran away screaming. James found it very upsetting.

Now one day, James decided to do something about it. So he invited all the townsfolk to a party. 'I can't make *little* cookies,' he explained on his invitation. 'So I'm afraid you'll have to make do with a *giant* sandwich instead.'

Everyone gathered in the town square. 'It's not a sandwich, but us that'll be on the menu,' said the mayor.

All the same, nobody dared to refuse the invitation. They all crept out of the town and up the hill to the giant's cave. There they could see James cutting up two enormous slices of bread.

'But what will the middle be?' asked the miller, anxiously.

Suddenly a delicious smell of strawberry jam came wafting down. The giant was making the town a huge jam sandwich.

'Yummy!' they all cried, and ran to join James for his party.

Pencil Sharpener

Rasheed's pencil needed
sharpening. So he twisted the pencil
in his dinosaur-shaped pencil
sharpener, until it had a lovely
sharp point.

Rasheed started to draw, but
the pencil lead was so long and thin
that it broke, and Rasheed had to sharpen the pencil all over
again!

Round and round went Rasheed's pencil in the dinosaur
sharpener until once again he had a lovely sharp point. Then
'crack!' the lead broke!

By the time Rasheed had sharpened it again, the pencil was
half the size.

'Gently,' said his teacher, 'or
you'll have no pencil left!'

This time Rasheed drew very,
very gently indeed, and finished his
picture – which was a drawing of a
very large dinosaur!

Photographs

Ben had a new camera. He liked taking pictures of all the family. Sometimes he was a bit impatient and took a picture of Mom with her eyes closed or Dad with only half an arm, but soon he had quite a collection – Mom, Dad, big sister Maria and baby Sarah. He even had one of the goldfish.

One day there was a school project. It was called 'My Family'. Ben thought and thought about what he could do. 'I could make a poster of the family pictures,' he suggested.

'I've an even better idea,' said Mom. 'Come with me.' Ben and Mom went up to the attic. Mom pulled out an old trunk and opened it. It was full of old photographs, some of them very faded and brown. 'This is me as a baby,' said Mom, 'and here's Dad on a school field trip. Oh, look! Grandma's wedding – and that's your Great-Grandad in his army uniform.'

'And *your* wedding, too,' said Ben, pointing to a picture.

'Why don't you make a family tree?' asked Mom. 'You can glue on a picture for each relative.'

So Ben and Mom gathered together a pile of pictures of Grandad, Grandma, Mom, Dad and all his aunts, uncles and cousins.

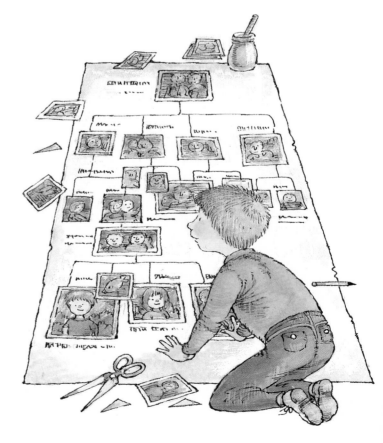

Then Ben took a huge sheet of paper. He printed Great-Great-Grandad's name on it and drew a line underneath with all his children's names. There was a picture for each member of the family even though some of them were rather fuzzy.

And right at the bottom were Ben's very own snapshots!

Garden Treasure

It was spring. Rasheed and Dad were in the yard. Rasheed was helping Dad to work in the vegetable patch.

'Wouldn't it be nice if we found some treasure,' said Rasheed, and just then, he dug up an old coin.

'There you are,' said Dad. 'Real treasure.'

'Is it gold?' asked Rasheed, hopefully.

'Clean it and see,' said Dad.

Rasheed took the coin to Mom. She began to rub it clean.

'Is it a gold coin?' asked Rasheed.

Mom burst out laughing. 'Not exactly. English, more like,' she said. 'It's an English pound coin. Dad must have dropped it when he came back from vacation there. But it's yours now.'

'I'll put it in a safe place,' said Rasheed. 'And perhaps one day I'll find some *real* treasure.'

Talking Doll

Angela had a talking doll. If you pulled a string in its back it would say, 'Hello, Mommy,' and sing, 'Ba-ba, black sheep'. Angela was thrilled about the doll. She kept pulling its string until the whole family was tired of its voice.

'I wish it could say something else,' grumbled her brother, Kevin. 'I'm sick of hearing "Ba-ba black sheep".'

'I'm sick of singing it,' said the doll.

Kevin gasped in astonishment.

'You can really talk!' said Angela.

'I say what children want to hear,' said the doll. 'And nobody in the toy store ever complained about "Ba-ba black sheep".'

'How about "Puddletown Fight Song"?' asked Kevin, who liked football.

'Or "We Three Kings"?' said Angela, who loved carols.

'I could do both,' said the doll. 'Football game one day, carols the next.'

And that's what happened. Kevin and Angela felt a bit silly carrying the doll to the football game, but everyone was *very* impressed by its enthusiasm as it cheered on the high school team.

And in church the next day, the whole congregation sat enchanted while a little doll-like voice soared to the rafters with the sound of 'We Three Kings'!

The Novelty Teapot

There was nothing Miss Wetherby liked more than a nice cup of tea. For years she had used the same brown teapot which had belonged to her mother before her. Then, one day, she broke the teapot. 'I must go out and buy another immediately,' said Miss Wetherby.

There was a special store in town that sold good tea and lots of different teapots.

'Now I *could* get another brown teapot,' said Miss Wetherby. 'But I think I'll get something really crazy.'

And do you know what she chose? A wonderful teapot shaped like a giraffe, with the spout at the end of his long neck and his tail curled to form a handle. And, what is more, Miss Wetherby swore that the tea tasted better from her giraffe teapot than from her ordinary old brown one!

The Fox and the Crow

Aesop

A crow once stole a piece of cheese and flew with it into a high tree. A fox was passing by at the time and his mouth watered at the sight of the cheese. 'But how can I make the crow drop it?' he wondered, and then he had a very clever idea.

'Crow,' called the fox. 'You are the most beautiful crow I have ever seen. Your feathers are glossy, your eyes are bright, and your talons must be the envy of every bird of prey. I'm sure that your voice must be equally magnificent.'

The crow was proud of such flattering remarks. He puffed out his chest, and opened his beak to show the fox what a wonderful caw he had. The piece of cheese fell on to the ground and was immediately snapped up by the fox!

The poor crow felt very foolish. He had been silly to listen to the crafty fox for it is well-known that there are many who will flatter and give false praise because they want something for themselves.

The Fisherman and the Little Fish

Aesop

A man once caught a tiny fish.

'I'm too small for a good meal,' pleaded the little fish. 'Throw me back and let me grow. I'll be a tasty mouthful next time I'm caught.'

This was the only catch the fisherman had made, and he wanted to return home with something. 'If I do what you ask I might never see you again,' he said. 'It's better to catch one small fish, than to hope for any number of large fishes.'

The Hen and the Golden Egg

Aesop

A woman had a hen that laid a golden egg each day. But the woman wasn't satisfied. 'One golden egg a day isn't really enough to become rich,' she complained.

So she killed the hen and cut it open, hoping to find a whole batch of golden eggs inside. Alas, there was nothing there at all! And now the woman had no hen and no golden eggs!

This sad tale proves that if you want more than you have already, you may end up with nothing!

The Pied Piper

Browning

Once upon a time there was a town in Germany that was plagued by rats. They ran everywhere – in the streets, in the houses, in the kitchens, and in the food itself. At last, the mayor of the town promised that whoever got rid of the rats would receive an enormous reward.

Very soon a strange-looking man appeared at the Town Hall. He was dressed in yellow and red, and he had a flute in his hand. 'Leave it to me,' he said. 'I will get rid of the rats.' The mayor agreed, and the Pied Piper played a strange little tune on his flute. Immediately, hundreds of rats tumbled out of every nook and cranny and followed the piper down to a river. They all jumped into the river and were drowned.

The mayor was delighted – but as he was very cheap he refused to give the Pied Piper his promised reward.

Then the Pied Piper put the flute to his lips, but this time all the children of the town followed him – deep into a mountain cave, where they all vanished, and were never seen again.

It is said that those children grew up, happy and carefree in a far off land, a long way away from the town with its cheap-minded mayor.

Car Washing

'Sarah, will you help me wash the car?' asked Dad one Saturday morning. Sarah was very willing. She fetched a bucket of soapy water and sponged the car all over.

'Now take the hose,' said Dad, 'and wash off all the soap.'

Dad climbed inside the car to clean off the seats, and Sarah attached the hose to a faucet. She turned it on, and swooshed the hose all over the car to remove the suds.

'Sarah!' roared Dad. 'What are you doing?' He climbed out of the car. He was drenched from head to foot.

Oh dear! Sarah had forgotten to close the car window!

'Next time,' said Dad grimly, 'you can do the inside!'

Farmyard Visit

The farm animals were furious. A group of school children had just visited the farm and they had been very bad. The cows had been teased, the sheep's wool had been pulled, and the ducks and chickens had been chased around the yard. And all the children had stared at them in a very rude manner.

'How would they like it if we visited them in their homes,' said Basil Bull.

'And pulled their hair,' added Emily Sheep.

Then Harry Horse had a very good idea. 'Let's go and visit those children,' he suggested. 'Let's stare at them and chase them round their yards.'

It all sounded great fun. Each animal chose a different child to visit and then they all set out for the town.

'Mom, there's a bull at the window!' screamed Sally. 'He's staring at me!'

'Shoo,' went Sally's mother, and Basil Bull moved off, trampling the tulips as he went. 'Help!' yelled Billy, as Henry Horse chased him all the way home from the mailbox. 'Ouch!' cried Peter, as a chicken pecked his leg. 'Don't do that!' shouted Mandy, as a sheep pulled her hair.

'Well, that should teach them a lesson,' said Basil Bull, as all the animals tramped back to the farm.

Later, all the children thought about how bad they had been on the farm, and how nasty it was to be treated the same way. And they never, ever, acted like that again!

Surprise Party

Samantha had invited ten friends to her birthday party. She was very excited about it. Just before the guests arrived her mother sent her to the supermarket to buy some candles for the cake.

'They'll all be there when I get back,' thought Samantha, skipping home. But when she arrived, there was no one there except Mom. 'My friends have forgotten to come!' wailed Samantha.

'Nonsense!' said Mom. 'They're all here if you look for them – let's play hide-and-seek, shall we?'

So Samantha looked in the hall closet and found Bill. She looked behind the sofa and found Clare. Tina and Laurie were behind the curtains and Tim was on the stairs. Very soon, all her ten guests had been found – together with the ten birthday presents they had brought her!

'This has been the best surprise party ever,' cried Samantha, before blowing out the candles on her cake.

The New Telephone

Mom was fed up with the old telephone. 'Every phone has buttons now,' she said. 'Not that silly dial.'

'And not that dull old black,' said John. 'There are hundreds of different colors to choose from.'

'Let's go and choose one, shall we?' said Mom.

So Mom and John went down to the store to look for a new phone. But when they reached the store there were so many different telephones that they did not know which one to buy. There was a round telephone and a pale pink one that hung on the wall. There was even one with a radio and alarm clock attached. Then John saw a wonderful telephone, shaped like Mickey Mouse.

'Can we have that one, Mom?' he pleaded. 'Please.'

Mom smiled. 'Why not?'

By the time they had left the store John was dreaming of a telephone of his very own – one that looked exactly like a racing car!

The Blacksmith's Silver

There once was a blacksmith who made very special horseshoes. These shoes were special because they were made from the finest silver.

One night a wicked thief stole the blacksmith's silver. The blacksmith didn't know what to do. Nobody wanted iron horseshoes from him, for you could get those anywhere. He was ruined! Just then, a beautiful young girl rode up on a white horse and asked for her animal to be shod in silver.

'Alas,' said the blacksmith, 'I'm afraid I cannot do it.' And he explained what had happened.

'Fill a jug with milk,' said the girl, 'and bring it to me.'

The blacksmith was mystified by her strange request, but he did as he was asked. The girl took the jug and poured the milk on to the anvil.

And before the astonished blacksmith could fetch a cloth to wipe it up, the spilled milk had changed into a big lump of silver!

The blacksmith set to work immediately to make the white horse's shoes, which were small and dainty, and unlike any he had seen before. Then the young girl sprang on to her horse and the blacksmith noticed that it had a long twirly horn, growing out of its forehead. It wasn't a horse at all – it was a unicorn!

The Duck Umbrella

Gemma was given an umbrella with a duck's head handle for her birthday. She was very proud of it.

The next day the sun was shining.

'Quack, quack, *quack*,' said the duck umbrella as Gemma put on her coat.

'I don't need you,' said Gemma. 'It's a sunny day.' But on the way home from shopping it poured and poured with rain. Gemma was soaked.

'I think that duck was telling me it would rain,' said Gemma. 'And I didn't take any notice.'

Gemma was right. Every time it was going to rain the duck umbrella would quack and Gemma would take it with her. And she never, ever, got wet again!

Twin Trouble

Sophy and Sharon were identical twins. They both had long dark hair cut in a fringe and brown sparkling eyes. No one could tell them apart. Now Sophy was tidy, quiet and good, while Sharon was untidy, noisy and very, *very* naughty. So they were different, really, inside.

You can imagine the sort of things that happened. Lots of the naughty things that Sharon got up to were blamed on Sophy, while Sharon was praised for something she hadn't done.

'That thoughtful little Sharon,' said an old lady, after Sophy had offered to carry her shopping home.

'That terrible Sophy!' said the vicar. 'I caught her swinging on my gate.'

Sophy thought it was all dreadfully unfair.

One day Mom took Sharon to the beauty parlor and had her hair cut short. 'Now you don't look exactly the same,' said Mom. Soon everyone knew that Sharon was the mischievous one with the short hair.

And, do you know, from that time on Sharon was never quite so naughty again. She wasn't *entirely* good – that would have been very boring, wouldn't it? – but certainly *better*. Sophy was also a little bit tired of being good – so, just sometimes, she too could be seen, swinging from the vicar's wooden gate!

Frog's Beauty Contest

All the frogs laughed at Fenella when they heard she had entered a beauty contest. 'Whoever heard of a beautiful frog?' they chortled.

'Fenella is *very* beautiful,' said her mother, 'for a frog.'

But that was the trouble. The beauty contest was not only for frogs, but for any animal that wanted to enter. There were robins, kittens, bullfinches and squirrels, and they had all spent hours grooming and preening themselves. Except for Fenella, for whoever had heard of a frog grooming itself?

The contest was to be held in Farmer Wurzel's field and judged by Oliver Owl. But on the day of the contest it poured and poured with rain. The field turned into one soggy, muddy mess and all the animals and birds became soaking wet. Except for Fenella. Her coat just shone and shone.

'Well,' said Oliver Owl, shaking his wet feathers. 'Brock Badger would have had the best coat if it wasn't covered with mud. And Roddy Robin *would* have had the finest red breast, if it wasn't so wet. In fact, the only animal who looks just as she should is the beautiful Fenella Frog!'

For Fenella's magnificent green skin glistened in the falling rain. She was undoubtedly the winner!

The King's Vacation

'I think I'll take a vacation,' said King Basil one day. 'But who will rule the kingdom while I'm away?'

'You'll have to advertise for someone,' said the queen.

So King Basil put a want ad in the City Gazette, but there were only three replies.

'That's not many,' said the queen.

'Well, it's not a job I'd like,' said the king.

'But you've got it,' pointed out the queen.

'Humph – but how nice it will be *not* to have it for two weeks.'

The first applicant didn't look very promising. He said he could make lots and lots of money.

'How?' asked the king, feeling very excited.

'By taxing the people,' replied the man.

'That's no good,' scoffed the king. 'The people would revolt and there would be no kingdom left for me to rule!'

The second didn't seem much better.

'I'm a soldier,' he said. 'I can win battles.'

'But we're not at war,' said the king, 'so that's no good.'

But the third man smiled broadly. 'I'll send everyone away on a two weeks' vacation,' he said. 'Then I'll have nobody to rule at all.'

'What an excellent idea,' said the king.

So the man ruled an empty kingdom while the people all joined King Basil on a wonderful vacation at the seaside.

Boris the Bat

Boris the Bat was looking for a new home.

'I don't want to live in any more dark belfries and dingy attics,' he said. 'I want somewhere bright and warm and cheerful.'

Boris searched high and low, but he still couldn't find exactly what he was looking for. Then one day he met Sally, who was walking home from school.

'Why don't you come and live in our classroom?' she asked. 'We're studying bats.'

So the very next day Boris the Bat went along to the school. There was a bright and cheerful classroom. There were the children with their nature notebooks. And there was a lovely wooden rafter from which Boris the Bat could hang!

'Welcome to your new home, Boris!' said the teacher.

Egg and Spoon Race

It was the school's sports day and Becky had entered the egg and spoon race.

'One, two, three, *go*,' said the principal, and they were off.

Three yards down the field Becky stumbled on a loose stone. The egg wobbled, but didn't fall. Becky held her arm very, very steady.

Six yards down the field, a dog ran out from the crowd. It snuffled round Becky's legs, but she walked on, and the egg stayed on the spoon.

Nine yards further on, the laces on Becky's trainers came untied. But Becky went on, slowly and carefully. The finishing line came nearer and nearer. Suddenly, Becky had won the race! 'Well done,' said the principal, handing her a prize. 'You didn't drop the egg once!'

The Dog and His Shadow

Aesop

A dog was walking along by a lake, with a piece of meat in his mouth. Suddenly he looked down and saw, reflected in the water, another dog who was also carrying a piece of meat.

'What a bit of luck,' thought the dog. 'If I can scare that fellow down there then I can have *two* pieces of meat.' So the dog barked fiercely and immediately the piece of meat he was carrying dropped from his mouth and sank in the waters of the lake.

However hard the dog tried, he could not retrieve it. Finally the dog slunk away, feeling very foolish. For as he had learned, if you try to take something that isn't really there, you may lose what you have already.

The Lion and the Mouse

Aesop

Once a lion was asleep when a mouse ran over his nose. The lion woke up immediately, and would have killed the little creature, but the mouse squeaked with fear, and pleaded for its life. The lion was a kind animal, despite his fierce appearance, so he set the mouse free. It ran off thankfully into the forest.

Some time later the lion was out hunting when he found himself entangled in a hunter's net. He roared and struggled, but the net pulled tighter and he knew he couldn't escape. Now the mouse heard the lion's roars, and he ran toward the animal who had once saved his life. Quickly he set to work, nibbling at the net until the lion was able to escape. So you see, the lion's kindness brought its reward.

The Three Kittens

There were once three naughty little kittens called Max, Emily and Fred. They all loved each other very much and when Mother Cat warned them that they would each have to find a separate new home and would never see each other again, they were furious.

'That won't do at all,' said Fred. 'We must *never* be parted.'

'But what shall we do?' squeaked Emily, who was the smallest kitten.

'We must make a plan to make sure someone takes us all,' said Max, who was black.

The very next day, two children came to choose a kitten with their mother. 'I'd like that tabby one,' said the little boy, pointing to Fred.

'No, no, that tiny orange one,' said the little girl, picking up Emily.

'Well, I like that black one,' said the Mother. 'I know, why don't we come back when we have made up our minds?'

While they were away, the kittens put their plan into action. They curled themselves up into a big ball of tabby, orange and black fur. You couldn't tell where one kitten began and the other ended.

When the Mother came back, she didn't have the heart to separate them, so she scooped up the sleeping ball of kittens and popped them all into the cat-basket.

Emily, Fred and Max yawned and stretched. Their trick had worked and they were all off to a new life together!

Playing Mailman

Jeremy's parents had given him a mailman's outfit for his birthday. It was very smart, with a blue peaked cap and a canvas postbag. The only trouble was, he didn't have any mail to deliver.

'Why don't you deliver my yard sale announcements?' asked Mom. 'Only down this street, though. I don't want you to cross the road.'

So Jeremy put the announcements into his canvas mail bag and set out. He delivered an annoucement to every house in the street. At No. 6 he was given a glass of milk and a chocolate cookie, but at No. 23 he was chased down the garden path by a shaggy brown dog!

'Phew!' said Jeremy, when he returned home. 'Now I really know what it's like to be a mailman!'

Snow-White

Grimm

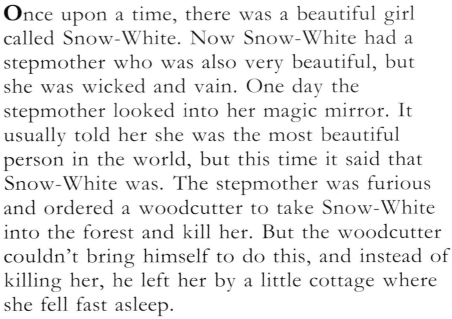

Once upon a time, there was a beautiful girl called Snow-White. Now Snow-White had a stepmother who was also very beautiful, but she was wicked and vain. One day the stepmother looked into her magic mirror. It usually told her she was the most beautiful person in the world, but this time it said that Snow-White was. The stepmother was furious and ordered a woodcutter to take Snow-White into the forest and kill her. But the woodcutter couldn't bring himself to do this, and instead of killing her, he left her by a little cottage where she fell fast asleep.

When she awoke, Snow-White found seven dwarfs looking at her. It was their cottage and they immediately took her in. Very soon, Snow-White was looking after them all and they loved her dearly.

When the wicked stepmother next consulted her mirror, she learnt that Snow-White was still alive. So she disguised herself as an old woman, and went to the cottage with a basket of poisonous apples. Snow-White ate one, and fell senseless to the ground. The evil stepmother was convinced she'd killed the girl.

The grieving dwarfs thought Snow-White was dead and put her in a glass coffin. On their way to the burial ground they met a prince, who asked to see the dead girl. The dwarfs set down the coffin. The movement jolted the poisoned apple out of Snow-White's mouth. She opened her eyes and immediately fell in love with the prince.

He carried her off to his kingdom and they lived happily ever after.

Potato Prints

'I think potatoes are boring,' said Matthew. He had just helped Dad dig up some potatoes from the vegetable patch.

'Useful things, potatoes,' said Dad. 'Boiled, fried or mashed.'

'Ugh!' said Matthew. 'I hate mashed potatoes!'

'Let me show you something interesting you can do with potatoes,' said Dad.

Matthew followed him into the kitchen. Dad cut a potato in half. Then he carved a daisy pattern on the cut side. He got a large sheet of white paper and mixed up some of Matthew's poster paints. He dipped the cut potato in the paint, and pressed it onto the paper.

'A daisy pattern,' said Matthew in delight. After that he made some more potato prints – an owl, a railway engine and a ship.

'Perhaps potatoes aren't so boring after all!' said Matthew.

The Special Present

Prince Jolly-Roger wanted to give his mother, Queen Seraphina, something special for her birthday. There were lots of things he *could* have bought her – treasure chests full of jewels, or a set of golden goblets – but when you are a queen these 'special things' are really rather ordinary.

So Prince Jolly-Roger searched the seven seas with his parrot and his cat looking for a gift, but not even a necklace of pearls seemed quite right.

Then, one day, the prince stopped off at a beautiful island. He was walking along a beach of silver sand, when he found a wonderful, curly shell with a pearly-pink inside. He lifted the shell to his ear and heard the sound of the sea.

'Mother always wanted to sail the seven seas,' said Prince Jolly-Roger. 'Now at least she can hear what it sounds like!'

Prince Jolly-Roger sailed for a week and a day until he reached his home. The queen's living-room was filled with flowers and precious gifts.

Beside these presents poor Prince Jolly-Roger's shell looked rather shabby. It also smelled of fish.

But the Queen loved his present most of all. For when she put the shell to her ear, she could dream of the sea.

The Hedley Kow

Jacobs

An old woman found a big black pot lying on the roadside. She picked it up and when she looked inside it was full of gold pieces. 'Well, that'll make me rich,' she exclaimed.

She started dragging the pot along, and then took another peep inside it. This time the pot was full of silver! 'Well,' said the old woman. 'Silver's less valuable than gold, so less likely to be stolen.'

The next time she looked, though, the silver had changed into iron! 'Iron is more useful than either gold or silver,' she said. But soon the iron had changed into a stone! 'Just right for keeping the door open,' she chuckled.

By now she had reached her gate, and she couldn't resist another peep at the pot. A huge dark shape leapt out of it. It had four legs, two long ears and a tail. 'Why,' cried the old woman. 'It's a Hedley Kow!' The Hedley Kow was a mischievous monster, though many doubted it existed at all.

'And I've seen it!' cried the old woman in amazement.

'What a very lucky person I am!'

The Zoo Attraction

The posters were going up all over the zoo. 'Arriving Saturday,' they said. 'New Attraction. Not to be missed.'

All the animals were very curious. 'I wonder what it can be?' they said. It was a small zoo but there were lots of animals there – lions and tigers, giraffes and elephants, polar bears, penguins, parrots and flamingos.

'It must be attractive if it's an attraction,' said Elephant.

'A panda, perhaps?' said Giraffe. 'Everyone loves pandas.'

'Or a gorilla,' shivered Chimpanzee with excitement. But he was a bit frightened, too.

'What *I'd* like to see,' said Penguin, 'is an albatross.'

On Saturday all the animals gathered to catch sight of the

new arrival. Two keepers brought in a big crate. They opened it, and out waddled the most peculiar-looking animal anyone had ever seen. It had a furry body like a bear, and a large beak rather like a duck's. The animals had never seen anything like it.

'What on earth *are* you?' asked Parrot, who wasn't known for his good manners.

'I'm a platypus,' said the creature. 'I come from Australia and don't know anyone here.'

The Gazelle burst into tears. 'How terribly sad and lonely for you,' he said.

And after that, all the animals made the platypus very welcome indeed, for it must be terrible to be the only one of your kind in a zoo.

Jack-in-the-Box

The Jack-in-the-box lived in the toy closet. Nobody had taken him out for a very long time. Marion didn't like opening the box. She didn't like Jack's ugly face springing up at her.

Poor Jack! He couldn't help being ugly. He couldn't help springing out of the box when it was opened. It was the way he was made.

One day, a little boy called Jake was playing with Marion, and he found the box. 'Don't open it!' cried Marion, putting her hands over her eyes. '*I hate* that old ugly Jack!'

Jake took no notice. He kept opening and shutting the box and Jack kept springing up and down until his poor ugly head spun. But then Jake opened the box once too often, and Jack's spring broke. Instead of leaping out of the box, Jack just sagged sadly over the edge.

Suddenly Marion felt very sorry for her poor Jack-in-the-box.

She gently took Jack off the broken spring. 'Mommy can make him into a puppet for me and I'll play with him every day,' she said.

And that is just what she did!

Park Playground

Sunita was taking her little brother, Prabir, to the playground. Prabir loved the playground, especially the merry-go-round. But today there were a lot of older boys there who were very noisy and were playing about on the slide. Sunita felt a bit frightened, but when she told Prabir she would like to feed the ducks instead, his face crumpled up and he started to cry.

'Want the merry-go-round,' he insisted.

Sunita looked across at the boys. They hadn't noticed her. She picked up Prabir and put him on the merry-go-round and very gently began to push him round. Prabir shouted and screamed with laughter.

'Hey, Kevin, let's try the merry-go-round,' shouted one of the boys. They all rushed over. They didn't seem to notice Sunita and Prabir. Kevin gave the merry-go-round one big push and wrenched it from Sunita's hand. Little Prabir went whizzing round on his own while the boys sprang on, laughing.

'*Be careful with my brother*,' cried Sunita. She was in tears. Prabir might fall off at any moment.

Then one of the big boys sat beside Prabir and held on to him. 'I'll take care of him,' he said. 'Look, he's loving it.'

And he was. With the big boy's arm tucked safely round him while the merry-go-round whizzed round and round, little Prabir was having the time of his life!

Under the Waterfall

'**I**'m going exploring,' said Grendel Goblin to Gerry. 'Do you want to come?'

Gerry had once set off to see the world, but he hadn't gone very far.

Grendel and Gerry took a train to the very foot of Humple-Dumple Mountain, and then started to walk.

'I'm so thirsty,' puffed little Gerry, as they began to climb. Grendel handed him a canteen of water. 'Don't drink too much, though,' he said. 'It has to last until we come back.'

Gerry took a sip, and then disaster struck! He dropped the canteen. The two goblins heard it bouncing down the mountainside and break on the rocks.

'You are careless, Gerry,' sighed Grendel. 'We'll just have to look for a mountain stream.'

On and on they climbed, higher and higher, getting thirstier and hotter all the time.

Suddenly the two goblins heard a distant roaring sound like thunder.

'It's an avalanche,' trembled Gerry.

'Don't be silly, there's no snow,' said Grendel. They climbed higher still, and there, far above them, they could see a sheet of water tumbling down.

'A waterfall,' cried Gerry and Grendel with relief. 'How wonderful!'

Both goblins ran toward it, bathing themselves in the torrent, and drinking the clear water.

'I *do* like exploring,' said Gerry.

Mouse in a China Store

One day Henry Mouse poked his nose out of his mousehole and into the store which he had explored so many times before. It was a candy store, and Henry always found something tasty to eat there. Today, though, he had a big surprise. Gone were the jars of brandyballs, the chocolate bars and the peppermint sticks. Gone, too, was the smell of candy.

Henry stood on his hind legs and jumped onto a shelf. There, face to face with him, was a cat. It was a very strange-looking cat, white with green flowers, and it was not much bigger than Henry himself. 'Call yourself a cat!' Henry jeered. He knocked it off the shelf and it crashed into tiny pieces on the floor. Next Henry climbed up a pink jar to look inside for chocolate drops. The jar tilted, and Henry went flying through the air as the jar fell. He ran here and there, sending displays of mugs, tea-services and crystal glasses flying everywhere. Then, suddenly, Henry smelt sugar. There, in a cracked dish he had just knocked over, was some pink and white candy. He licked one – delicious! Henry Mouse crept back into his hole again, a sugared almond in his mouth.

'These won't last long,' said Henry. 'I'll look for a new home tomorrow!'

The Windmill

There was once an old windmill that stood on a hill. Its sails were broken and it was many years since it had been used. It was very lonely, and it longed for the sound of human voices.

One day it heard some children playing outside. 'We're going to live here,' one of them said.

The windmill couldn't believe what it had heard. Surely children weren't strong enough to grind the grain? But later, some workmen arrived. The old windmill was hammered and painted and tidied up. Soon it was a cosy home for the children and their parents, and though its sails never turned, the windmill wasn't lonely any more.

The Three Little Pigs

Traditional

Once upon a time there were three little pigs, and each of them built a house. The first little pig built his house out of straw, and very smart it was too. The second little pig built his house out of wood. But the third little pig built his house out of brick. And though the house was plain it was very sturdy.

Presently, along came a wicked old wolf. The three little pigs rushed into their homes. But with a huff and a puff the wolf blew down the straw house and gobbled up the first little pig. Then he went to the second little pig's house. He huffed and he puffed, and he blew down the wooden house, and gobbled up the second little pig.

Then up to the brick house came the wicked old wolf. But though he huffed and puffed until he had no breath left, he could not blow it down. The wicked old wolf slunk away, very disappointed. He was never seen in those parts again and the third little pig lived in his strong, plain house to the end of his days.

The Dancing Hippo

Belinda had always wanted to be a ballet dancer. It's the dream of many a small girl, but Belinda was different. Belinda was a hippopotamus!

'Don't be silly,' said her mother. 'Hippos don't dance. You'd break the stage.'

Belinda looked all over the country for a ballet school, but none of them would take a hippo. Only humans were meant to dance, it seemed.

'There's only one thing to do,' said Belinda. 'I'll start my own ballet company. So Belinda formed the BBC – which stood for Belinda's Ballet Company. It was just for hippos, and it was a huge success. It was surprising how many hippos there were who wanted to dance!

Piggy Bank

The china piggy bank was very handsome, but he wasn't happy. He wanted to meet some real pigs.

So, one day, Piggy bank jumped from the window-sill and set out. Very soon he came to a farmyard, and he could see some very large and very dirty animals snuffling into their trough. 'What funny creatures,' thought Piggy bank. 'I wonder what they are?'

'Pigs, of course,' said one of the animals. 'And what are you?'

'I'm a pig too,' said Piggy bank.

'But you're covered in pink flowers,' said a pig, 'and you've got a slot in your back.' And all the pigs laughed at him.

Piggy bank trotted sadly back to his window-sill. And there was something waiting for him – a blue glass pig. Piggy bank had found a friend!

Bookworm

Charlie loved going to the library. 'He's a proper bookworm,' said Mom. 'Dives into every book he can get his hands on.'

One day, Charlie was standing by the shelves wondering what he could take out, when a little voice suddenly said: 'Why don't you try "*Mystery at Hollyhock Farm*"?'

Charlie turned round – but there was nobody there.

'Here I am,' said the voice again. It came from the shelf. Charlie peered more closely and saw a very tiny black and white worm staring back at him with bright eyes. 'I'm a bookworm,' it explained. 'I just love words.'

Charlie pulled out the book the bookworm had told him to read.

'But it's got no words in it,' he exclaimed.

'I know – I've eaten them,' said the bookworm. 'You could write in your own words,' it said helpfully, 'if I tell you the story.'

'But this is *terrible*,' said Charlie. 'If you eat all the words nobody can enjoy the books.'

The bookworm started to cry. 'But I live on words,' he said. 'What can I do?'

Charlie thought hard. 'I know,' he said. 'I'll bring you all Dad's old newspapers. You can eat them instead.'

This seemed to be a very good idea. So, each time he went to the library, Charlie would take piles of old newspapers and the bookworm ate all the words. Sometimes Charlie forgot, so if you ever go to the library and find a book with no words in it, you'll know exactly what happened.

Tea-Party Witch

Miranda knew that Miss Stone was a witch even if she didn't look like one. She had a black cat, a cauldron and a black sack full of magic. Miranda had seen her carrying them all into the house on the day she moved in. And today she was coming to her Mom's tea-party!

Miss Stone arrived in an elegant cream-colored dress and a big floppy hat. She sat daintily on the edge of her chair, and nibbled some sandwiches. Miranda thought she must have made a mistake. But then Miss Stone suddenly leapt to her feet and pointed toward the sky.

'Bother that cat!' she cried. 'I told it to stay at home.'

Miranda looked out of the window and had a shock. There was Miss Stone's black cat, sailing over the treetops on a broomstick!

Garden Pond

Matthew wanted to have a pond. His dad had a good idea. He went to a store and bought the biggest plastic tub he could find. Then he dug a hole in the yard and sank the tub into it. 'Now fill it with water,' he said. After that, Dad and Matthew bought some fish weed and a plastic basket with a water lily in it. They sank it all in the pond, and later they added some frogs' eggs.

One day Matthew went to look at his pond and saw a tiny frog sitting on a lily pad!

The Bonfire

It was the fall and the yard was covered with fallen leaves.

'Will you help me sweep them up, Steve?' asked Dad. 'Then we can make a bonfire.'

So Steve and Dad swept up a pile of leaves as tall as Steve. Then Dad added some tree branches that had been blown down in a big storm.

'Now we'll light the bonfire,' he said.

It was an enormous bonfire. Steve and his friend, Jill, from next door, danced round it. Then Mom let them have a couple of potatoes wrapped in tinfoil and Dad poked them into the hot embers.

'Baked potatoes – yummy!' said Steve. The bonfire was worth all the hard work.

The Ticklish Dragon

Giles was a perfectly ordinary dragon. He had lots of green scales, and breath as hot as a furnace. But one day while Giles was walking in the meadow, minding his own business, he heard the sound of thundering hoofbeats. A knight was galloping toward him, lance at the ready. What was worse was that the knight was St George.

'This is the end of me,' thought Giles, who wasn't very brave. Just then, St George's lance glanced off his scales. It didn't hurt Giles, but it did tickle him – and Giles was *very* ticklish! 'He, he, he,' giggled Giles.

St George tried again and then again, but each time his lance just slid down Giles's scales, tickling him terribly.

Now St George was used to two sorts of dragon: the fierce, fiery sort, and the cowardly ones who ran away. He had never, ever met a giggly one before.

Soon St George had to give up. He could no more kill a giggly dragon rolling on his back than he could kill his own pussy cat. He galloped away, leaving Giles doubled-up with laughter.

And so it was that Giles, the ticklish dragon, defeated the master dragon-slayer, St George.

Goblin Races

Griselda Goblin was preparing her mouse for the Races. She brushed its fur until it shined like brown velvet.

'I've heard,' said Gareth Goblin, 'that Garth Goblin's rat is racing.'

'That's not fair,' said Griselda. 'A rat's much bigger than a mouse. It's sure to win.'

Sure enough, Garth's rat was waiting at the starting line. It was enormous!

The starting whistle went, and the animals were off! Garth's rat was soon in trouble. Because he was so large, he kept stumbling over the little mice scurrying along. And as he was so fat, he was soon huffing and puffing and slowing down.

'My mouse has won,' cried Griselda at the end of the race.

'Bah!' snarled Garth in disgust.

'There's no doubt,' said Griselda, 'that biggest does not necessarily mean best!'

The New Dog

Darrel wanted a dog. At first his parents said no. They said his little sister Sue was too young; they said a dog would make a mess around the house. But then, on his seventh birthday, Darrel had the most wonderful surprise.

'Let's go to the Dogs' Home,' said Mom and Dad, 'and find you a puppy.'

So Mom, Dad, Darrel and little Sue set off to the Dogs' Home. Dad and Sue waited in reception, while Mom and Darrel went to choose a dog.

Darrel found it difficult to decide which one to take. First, he wanted a pretty little white fluffy dog, then an ugly old black one that no one else would want. Next, he fell for a big, bouncy Irish Wolfhound, which Mom said was too big, and a shivering little puppy that Mom said looked too nervous and delicate.

'I want them all,' said Darrel in despair.

Finally, they came to a cage full of half-grown puppies with brown shaggy hair and long legs. One of the puppies came bouncing up to the wire and scrabbled and whined at Darrel.

He had huge amber-colored eyes and as soon as he saw him, Darrel knew it was the right puppy.

'That's the one I want,' said Darrel, 'because he's chosen *me*.'

Playing Beauty Parlor

Alice's friend, Tessa, was coming over to play. Tessa had been
to Alice's lots of times before. She had played with all Alice's
toys and games and had tried on all her clothes.

'Let's do something different,' she suggested.

Alice was a bit frightened of Tessa. Sometimes she wished
she wasn't her friend at all. 'Let's go to Mom's room,' said Alice.
But as soon as Tessa went in there, she cried: 'Make-up, and hair
gel!' She ran straight to the dressing-table and smothered hair gel
all over her hair. Then she squirted some mousse on the carpet.
Finally, she tied up her hair with all Mom's prettiest ribbons and
bows. By the time she had finished there was an awful mess
everywhere.

'Alice! Tessa!' Mom had come up to call them for a snack.
She stood looking at the mess.

'Clean all this up,' she said. 'And then Tessa can go straight
home. No milk and no special cookies!'

Alice knew Tessa wouldn't be asked again. She was quite
pleased about this. Tessa was very bossy. Mandy next door was
much nicer!

The Ugly Duckling

Andersen

There was once a duck who had a whole family of ducklings. They were fluffy, pretty little things – except for one. He was large, gray and scrawny. All his brothers and sisters laughed at him until he swam away, unable to bear their unkindness.

Everywhere the duckling went it was the same. 'Shoo,' people would say. 'Go away, you ugly thing.' Everywhere he went the duckling was chased, scolded and laughed at.

One day he saw two graceful swans gliding on a lake. 'If only I were beautiful like those swans,' he thought.

Then one of the swans came swimming across the water to him. 'Welcome, brother,' he said.

'Brother?' said the duckling. 'But I'm not a swan, I'm an ugly duckling.'

'Ugly indeed!' said the swan. 'Have you looked at yourself?'

The duckling looked at his reflection in the water – and what did he see but a beautiful white swan looking back at him!

The ugly duckling was so happy that he forgot how miserable he had been. He stayed with his new friends and glided across the lake into the sunset. And he was never called ugly again.

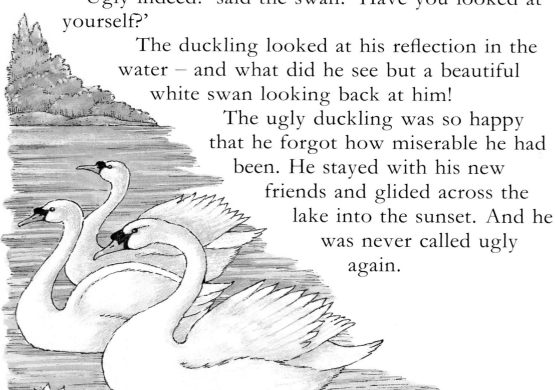

The Dish and the Spoon

Hey diddle, diddle
The cat and the fiddle,
The cow jumped over the moon;
The little dog laughed
to see such sport,
and the dish ran away with the spoon.

Have you ever wondered what happened to the dish that ran away with the spoon?

The dish was rather pretty with yellow daffodils and violets painted on it. The spoon was strong, plain and very useful.

At first, the dish was glad to have such a sensible companion, for it was thin and able to slip into kitchens

to find spoonfuls of food for them both.

But then the dish met a more beautiful blue and white Chinese bowl. The dish talked and talked with the bowl and soon they were the best of friends.

The spoon felt sad at first, but just afterwards it met a delightful silver knife, and then the four friends lived together happily ever after.

Pelican Shopper

Mrs Marvel had a very unusual pet. It was a pelican. It ate lots and lots of fish, and people would often ask her why she kept such a peculiar and expensive bird.

'A parakeet would be more sensible,' said one neighbor.

'Or a canary,' said another.

'I do wish people would mind their own business,' thought Mrs Marvel, and she decided to show them what her pelican could do.

The next day, Mrs Marvel went to the supermarket with her pelican instead of her shopping basket. She bought two fish, two cans of fruit, a can of coffee, six oranges and a jar of jam. And do you know where she put all these things? Why, in the pelican's enormous beak, of course!

The Magic Rocking Chair

One Christmas, Dad brought an old rocking chair home from a junk store. It had strange stars carved along its top and dragons' heads on its arms.

Rachel sat in it at once, and started to rock backward and forward. 'I bet it's magic,' she thought. And so it was. The chair rocked faster and faster and then, suddenly, it took off into the air. It flew out of the window and up to the stars. Rachel closed her eyes and hung on for dear life. When she looked again, the chair was flying past a star. 'I do believe I could catch it,' thought Rachel. So she reached out and took it in her hand. It felt cold, like an icicle, but it didn't melt.

'How dare you steal my star?' roared a voice from nowhere.

Rachel was very scared. She stared into the darkness. 'Who are you?' she asked fearfully.

'I am the Star Dragon,' replied the voice. Rachel saw two huge eyes glaring at her like live coals. She was just about to return the star, when the chair started to descend. Rachel felt funny, like going down in an elevator very fast . . .

'Wake up, Rachel,' came her mother's voice. Rachel opened her eyes. She was sitting safe and sound in the rocking chair by the fire. But in her hand was a little, shining star.

Old Sid's Goose

Old Sid lived alone in the middle of the country. He lived simply, but some said he had a fortune tucked away in his cottage. As the years went by, the rumors about Sid's fortune grew. Some claimed he had diamonds, others said he had golden goblets. Bert the burglar listened to these tales and grew more and more excited. He had often seen Old Sid in the village. He was always alone, with not even a dog to guard him. 'I think I'll go along and see what I can steal,' said Bert to himself.

So, just as dusk was falling, Bert sneaked along to Old Sid's cottage. A light shined in the cottage window.

Bert crept up the path. Suddenly, he heard a terrible hissing sound. Something large and white was advancing toward him – something was flapping its enormous wings.

'Ooh,' cried Bert. 'It's a ghost!' Bert fled back toward the gate, but as soon as he felt a sharp nip on the back of his legs, he knew what the ghost was. Old Sid had a goose, and a goose is fiercer than the fiercest watchdog!

Old Sid chuckled. 'Another thief after my fortune,' he said as he made some tea in the one treasure he possessed – his grandmother's old silver teapot!

Fishing Trip

Ben, Briony, Mom and Dad were on vacation by the seaside. Briony was upset. She had lost one of her favorite sandals.

'Don't worry,' said Dad. 'Let's go fishing to cheer you up.'

They hired a small boat and the family were soon way out to sea beyond the bay. They all got out their fishing lines.

Very soon, Mom had caught a plaice, Dad had caught a crab, Briony had landed a herring and Ben – why Ben caught Briony's missing sandal!

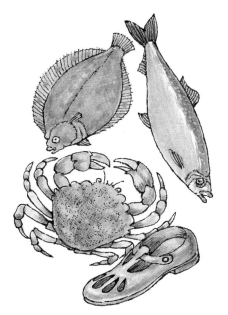

Paddy the Puppet

Paddy the Puppet lay in the middle of a jumble sale booth. He was unable to move because his strings were missing. Several children picked him up, then threw him down again in disgust.

Paddy was worried. If no one bought him by the end of the sale, he knew he would be taken to the dump.

Suddenly a woman picked him up. 'Look at this puppet, Emma,' she said to her daughter. 'I remember having a puppet theater when I was small. If we could fix some new strings onto this one, you can start your own puppet theater.'

And so it was that Paddy became the first puppet in Emma's new collection!

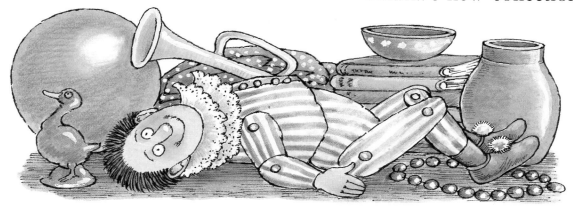

Goblin Treasure Hunt

Grendel Goblin was organizing a treasure hunt through Peppercorn Wood. Every goblin had to follow a trail of real acorns, which would lead them to the prize: a solid silver acorn cup. But the treasure hunt was a huge flop.

'I can't find one single acorn,' complained Gareth Goblin.

'Nor me,' said Griselda. And nor could any of the other goblins.

Grendel Goblin was puzzled. It hadn't been a very difficult treasure hunt. In the end he had had to give the silver acorn cup to the goblin who had walked the farthest.

The very same day, Joey Squirrel was having the feast of his life.

'All that food!' he sighed. 'Just laid out, all ready for me!' And he curled up happily with his huge store of acorns.

Bruno the Junk Store Bear

Bruno the wooden bear stood outside Mr Carter's junk store. He was enormous. Most of the children were frightened of Bruno, but Jason loved him. If he stood on tip-toe, he could reach right inside Bruno's open mouth.

One night Mr Carter was burgled. The burglars stole some old jewelry from a special show-case. Luckily, a policeman was passing the store just as the burglars rushed out. The burglars tried to run away, but they stumbled against Bruno, and the policeman caught them red-handed.

'It's very funny, though,' said Mr Carter to Jason the next day. 'I've found all the jewelry except for a jade bracelet. I wonder what the burglars did with that?'

Jason had an idea. He put his hand into Bruno's mouth.

'I've found it, Mr Carter,' he said. 'They hid it in Bruno's mouth!'

'Clever old Bruno,' said Mr Carter. 'And clever Jason too. The burglars must have put it there, hoping to collect it when they came out of prison. Well, I can't give Bruno a reward, but I can give you one.'

And he gave Jason a beautiful old box camera. Jason was thrilled and immediately took a photo of Bruno and Mr Carter outside the junk store.

The Old Man and his Donkey

Aesop

An old man and his son were taking a donkey to market. They had not gone far along the road when a passer-by called out to the father: 'Why let your son walk, when he could ride on the donkey?'

So the old man put the boy on the donkey's back, and off they went again.

Very soon someone else cried out to the boy: 'Imagine letting your old father walk while you ride, you lazy boy!'

'How right you are,' said the man. He then climbed up behind his son, and off they went, riding together.

'You do see some cruel sights,' they heard someone remark, as they traveled on. 'That poor beast is so overloaded that its legs are quite bent.'

'Well, there's only one thing left to do,' sighed the man, and he tied the donkey to a pole, and both father and son walked into town, carrying the donkey between them. Of course, they looked so silly that everyone laughed their heads off. The old man was so furious that he let the donkey loose in a field, and returned home with his son.

If you try to please everyone, you end up pleasing nobody at all.

The Ant and the Grasshopper

Aesop

There was once a grasshopper who sang all the summer through, completely forgetting that winter was approaching.

That winter was very cold and the grasshopper was soon starving. 'I know,' he said. 'I'll ask the ant for some food. I know he has a store of grain he's saved from the summer.'

When the grasshopper saw the ant he begged him for some food. But all the ant said was: 'I was busy preparing for winter while you were singing. Why should I help you now? May I suggest that as you spent the summer singing, you can't do better than spend the winter dancing?' And he laughed and went on with his work.

So the poor grasshopper starved, because he had idled away the summer without thought of the winter ahead.

Walter the Express Train

Walter was an express train, who rushed at over 100 miles per hour. Walter was very proud of his speed. He overtook cars and trucks and slow trains and rushed through stations and tunnels.

Every day Walter would pass Sam the stopping train. He would hoot loudly and call out, 'Slowcoach!'. But Sam didn't mind. He preferred to trundle along, picking up passengers at every station. He was a friendly little train.

One morning, just after he had hooted at Sam on his way to New York, Walter broke down, right at the end of the station platform. Everyone got out, stamping their feet angrily in the cold. 'Stupid train,' they said. 'So unreliable.'

Walter was towed into a siding. He watched as Sam chunted into the station.

'Hurrah,' cried the passengers from the express train. 'You've rescued us!' and they all climbed aboard.

Later Walter was on his way again, but he was nearly empty. Even the restaurant car had closed down.

'I'll never laugh at Sam again,' said Walter. 'Who knows, one day I may be able to help him out.'

Space Chase

Paul was sitting in his space suit watching a science fiction movie on television. 'The astronauts are being chased by alien spaceships,' said Paul. 'They need some extra help.'

Suddenly, the spaceship's Captain reached out a hand from the television screen. 'Quick, Paul,' he said. 'Come and help us!'

Paul sprang to his feet and stepped through the screen. He was there, among the aliens and the spaceships. On the Captain's instructions, Paul helped steer the spaceship away from the aliens and back to Earth.

When it was all over, Paul stepped back into his living-room. Had it really happened? Or was it a dream? Then the Captain's face appeared on the screen.

'Thanks, Paul,' he said.

Penguin Fashion

'You look very nice,' said Mrs Penguin to her son, Harold.

'I don't want to look nice,' said Harold. 'I look stupid dressed up in this black and white outfit. It's so old-fashioned.'

'Please yourself,' snapped his mother.

So Harold did. First, he painted his white chest with blue paint. Then, he carefully painted his flippers bright red. 'Dead trendy,' he said to himself, as he marched off to the penguin pool to visit his friends.

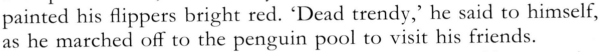

All his friends fell about laughing. 'Call yourself a penguin,' they jeered. 'You look more like a dressed-up toucan!'

Poor Harold! He was so embarrassed he dived into the pool – and when he came up again he was a black and white penguin once more!

The Terrible Trumpet

Andrea's mother gave her a trumpet for her birthday. There was a booklet with the trumpet, telling you how to play it, but Andrea didn't bother with this. 'I can pick it up as I go along,' she said.

By the end of the day, her mother wished she had given Andrea a stamp album instead. By the end of the week, the next door neighbors had put a 'For Sale' sign on their house, and by the end of the month, the dog had moved out to the shed. Only the cats seemed to like the trumpet. They sang to its music.

'If you don't learn to play that trumpet properly, I'll throw it away!' said her mother.

She made Andrea follow the instructions in the booklet and very soon Andrea was able to play 'The Star Spangled Banner' with barely a wrong note. The neighbors had moved out by this time, but a music teacher had moved in instead!

And now Andrea is the chief trumpet-player in the school band, and on the Fourth of July all the school will march in the town parade to the sound of Andrea's trumpet!

Dennis the Donkey

Ever since he won the donkey derby, Dennis the Donkey had been quite impossible. He spent all his time boasting about how quickly he could run. 'I'm the fastest donkey in the country,' he would say. 'And next year – you wait – I'll be the fastest donkey in the world.'

All that summer Dennis basked in his own glory. He didn't bother to run round the field with the other donkeys. He didn't offer to pull the children around the farm in the little cart. And when some of the donkeys went off to give donkey rides, Dennis was nowhere to be seen. 'I'm saving my strength for next spring,' he said. But Dennis grew very fat and lazy. He spent his days grazing and munching carrots.

When donkey derby day came round the following spring, Dennis proudly waddled off to the starting line. I need hardly tell you that he didn't stand a chance. He had barely gone a hundred yards before he was completely out of breath. By the time he finished he was third from last, and all he wanted to do was to collapse in a nice shady corner.

'Ha, ha,' laughed the other donkeys. 'The fastest donkey, eh? The *fattest*, more like!'

Grandfather Clock

There was once a grandfather clock with no voice. Years ago someone had removed it because they didn't like his chiming in the middle of the night. Now he stood in a corner, silent and dusty.

One day an old man came to stay and he spoke to the grandfather clock. 'Hello, old friend,' he said. 'I remember you when I was a boy. I learned to count by your chimes. How sad that you've lost your voice.'

That night the old man couldn't sleep. The house seemed strange without the chiming clock. 'Do get it fixed,' he said to his daughter the next day. 'It's the heartbeat of the house.'

And so she did. The grandfather clock got his voice back once again.

Castle in the Mist

Dad, Briony and Ben were out for a walk when the mist came down.

'We're lost,' wailed Ben, who wasn't very brave.

'We'll be all right if we keep on the path,' said Dad. 'We may spot a landmark further on.'

'I can see a castle,' said Briony.

'Don't be stupid,' said Ben. 'There aren't any castles round here.'

'It's got towers,' said Briony. 'I can see them.'

Ben looked hard and saw, in the distance, something that looked like a castle.

'Perhaps it's guarded by a fierce dragon,' said Ben fearfully.

Suddenly, Dad burst out laughing. 'It isn't a castle. It's the old cement factory. It looks far more romantic in the mist.'

But Ben walked by the 'castle' on tiptoe – just in case!

Supermarket Thief

Le Wong loved going to the supermarket with his mom. He liked pushing the cart along. But Le Wong was a great dreamer. One day he completely forgot he was pushing a supermarket cart. He thought he was driving a chariot. He charged down the aisles, tipping over piles of cans.

'Catch that child,' roared the manager angrily.

'Come here, Le Wong,' called his mother. But Le Wong didn't hear either of them.

Down by the check-out counter, a young man was sneaking out with a dozen packs of cigarettes under his coat. Le Wong came racing along, and knocked him sideways. Cigarettes went flying in all directions.

'Congratulations,' said the manager. 'You've caught the supermarket thief. You can come and race our carts any time you like!'

Unmatched Socks

It was a dark winter morning and Paul had overslept. As he groped for his clothes, he put them on any old way, and then rushed outside. But when he climbed on to the school bus, everyone started to snigger. What was the matter?

At school, Paul walked across the playground with his friend, Terry. Terry was trying hard not to laugh.

Then his teacher said, 'You've got unmatched socks on!' And so he had – one blue and the other yellow!

Tamlane

Jacobs

A young man called Tamlane once fell in love with a girl named Janet. But before they could get married, Tamlane was stolen by the fairies, for the Fairy Queen wanted Tamlane to be her Knight.

Some days later, Tamlane managed to snatch a meeting with Janet, and tell her how to rescue him. Janet remembered everything he said. The next day she hid herself and waited for the Fairy Queen to ride by with Tamlane.

As soon as she saw him, Janet sprang up and snatched Tamlane from his saddle, hugging him tight. The fairies tried every spell under the sun to release him. They turned him to ice, and then to fire, they changed him into a snake and after that a swan. But Janet did not let go of him, however much he froze and burned and struggled in her arms.

Finally, with a wail of rage, the Fairy Queen rode away with her courtiers. Tamlane turned back into his proper shape again and was Janet's true love for ever.

Crocodile Ferry

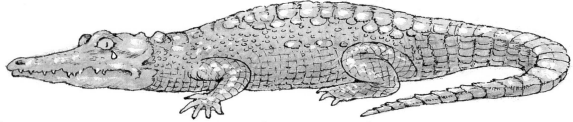

'**N**obody likes me,' complained the crocodile.

'That's because you're so nasty,' replied the monkey. 'You always snap at everyone with those sharp teeth of yours.'

'It's my nature,' said the crocodile. 'But it would be nice to be popular and to have some friends,' he added wistfully.

'There's one thing that you could do,' said the monkey. 'During the monsoon rains our little stream becomes a river. Some of the smaller animals can't get across. If you turn yourself into a crocodile ferry, you'll be very popular.'

So when the monsoon came, the crocodile stood at the edge of the river and waited for his passengers. Some were a bit frightened at first – and who wouldn't be! Would you like to cross the river on a crocodile's back? But at last a porcupine bravely jumped on and the crocodile swam with him safely to the other side. After that, everyone used the crocodile ferry.

Soon the crocodile was one of the most popular animals in the jungle. And though he was sometimes tempted to snap up a tasty morsel, he never did, for he always remembered how very nice it was to have so many friends.

King of the Jungle

The tiger and the monkey were arguing over who was the King of the Jungle. 'I'm the King of the Jungle,' said the tiger. 'Everyone knows that I'm big and fierce and very clever.'

'But I'm more agile,' said the monkey. 'And I can climb trees.'

'Pooh, what's the use of that!' jeered the tiger.

Then, one day, the tiger's little cub went missing. The tiger and the tigress searched for him everywhere, but no one could find him.

'I'll look for you,' said the monkey kindly, forgetting their quarrel.

He climbed up the highest tree in the jungle and looked far into the distance. A long way away, he could see a tiny object with yellow and black stripes moving across a clearing. 'I think I've found him!' he told the tiger. He couldn't help adding: 'Climbing trees sometimes has its uses, don't you think?'

The Seagull's Friend

Cedric the Seagull's best friend was the lighthouse keeper, Bill. When the weather grew cold and rough, Cedric would fly out to sea to the lighthouse and perch on the gallery.

'Let me in, I'm cold,' Cedric would cry, and Bill would let him into the room, and feed him on fresh mackerel.

But one winter morning Bill did not open the window when Cedric tapped on it. Cedric looked through the little curved window, and was shocked to see Bill lying on the ground with a twisted leg.

'I must get help quickly,' said Cedric.

So he flew back to the little harbor, perched on the harbor-master's shoulder and shrieked in his ear. Then he flew off to the lantern at the end of the pier and looked toward the lighthouse and flapped his wings.

'I believe that seagull wants me to visit the lighthouse,' said the harbor-master, and he jumped into his little rowing-boat and set out to sea.

Sure enough, when he arrived, he found poor Bill lying there with a broken leg. 'I fell down the spiral staircase,' said Bill. 'And if it wasn't for Cedric I'd be lying there still!'

Princess Scatterbrains

There once was a very absent-minded princess. In fact, she was so absent-minded that the king and queen despaired of ever finding her a husband. 'She'll forget her own name next,' sighed the queen, as the princess went to find her best pearl crown which she had left hanging on a willow tree by the river.

And indeed, though many princes came and went, none of them seemed very eager to marry a girl who wore unmatched socks to the state banquet.

But one day a very strange-looking man turned up and asked to marry the princess. He had a patch over one eye, and a parrot perched on his shoulder. In fact he looked exactly like a pirate. 'I think I can cure the princess of her scatterbrained ways,' said Prince Jolly-Roger. 'And I really would like to marry her – if she'll have me.'

The princess agreed at once, for what could be more exciting than marrying a pirate? The two of them traveled the seven seas on Prince Jolly-Roger's ship. He even cured Princess Scatterbrains of her absent-mindedness. The parrot would perch on the princess's shoulder and every now and again would shriek in her ear: 'Have you forgotten something?' It was the only phrase the parrot knew – but it did the trick!

Goblin Clown

Gareth the Goblin wanted to be a clown. He painted his face white, drew red circles around his eyes, and practiced standing on his head. But Grendel wasn't impressed.

'You don't make me laugh,' he said.

Gareth threw a custard pie at Garth, the grumpy goblin. But Garth wasn't amused. 'I thought clowns were meant to be funny,' he said.

So Gareth put on a big false nose like an oversized cherry.

'You look stupid,' said Griselda.

'I'm a failure,' wailed Gareth, and he stomped off down the street. Outside the store, he slipped on a banana peel.

'Ha, ha, ha,' laughed Grendel and Griselda. 'Sorry for laughing, but you do look funny!'

Grandfather's Pigeon

Susie's grandfather kept pigeons which he entered in races. His champion was a big pigeon with a green collar. But Susie's favorite was a light gray and white bird with bright, friendly eyes called Silver.

One day Susie found Grandfather looking up at the sky. 'Silver's missing,' he said. 'He didn't come back after the last race.'

Susie was heartbroken. She went round to her Grandfather's house every day to see if Silver had returned. Every day she looked up into the sky, hoping.

Then, one day, Susie had to take her cat to the vet. While she was waiting a boy came in, carrying a cardboard box. He sat down next to Susie.

'Don't let your cat eat my pigeon,' he joked. 'The vet's just fixed his broken wing.'

'May I see him?' asked Susie. 'I love pigeons.'

The boy opened the box a crack. Susie peered in. It was Silver.

'I found him a few weeks ago, with a broken wing,' said the boy, 'and the vet's fixed it for me.'

Susie explained what had happened. 'But I don't think Silver will be any good for racing now,' she said. 'Perhaps Grandfather will let you keep him.'

And Grandfather did. Susie made friends with the boy, and she saw Silver every single week.

The Secret Tide Pool

On the last day of Ben and Briony's seaside vacation, Ben decided to go exploring on his own. When Mom and Dad weren't looking he started to climb over the rocks at the edge of the bay. There he found a beautiful tide pool hidden deep in a rock basin. It was full of bright green seaweed and red sea anemones that waved their tentacles in the still, clear water. Under a big stone a little crab was burying itself in the sand.

Ben sat there, looking at the pool, for a long time. It was very peaceful and secret. Suddenly, he heard Dad's voice. 'Ben, Ben, where are you?'

Ben tried to pretend he hadn't heard. Then Dad's head appeared over the rocks.

'Come along at once, Ben,' he ordered. 'Can't you see what's happening?'

Ben looked. The sea had crept right up. It was too deep for him to wade back again.

'Right,' said Dad. 'Piggy-back.'

Ben climbed onto Dad's back. Dad waded across to the beach. When Ben looked back a little later he couldn't see the rocks at all. His secret tide pool lay hidden, deep in the sea.